EARL OF DARBY

(ONCE UPON A WIDOW #4) (WICKED EARLS' CLUB
ROUND 2)

AUBREY WYNNE

DEDICATION

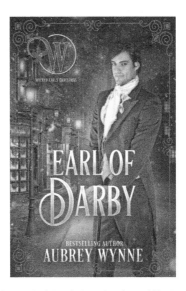

To the wonderful and talented authors of The Wicked
Earls' Club: I am honored to be a part of this unique
series. I have found my niche and will be forever grateful.

ISBN: 978-1-946560-19-3

❦ Created with Vellum

PROLOGUE

There is a fountain fill'd with blood
Drawn from Emmanuel's veins;
And sinners, plung'd beneath that flood,
Lose all their guilty stains.

> — *"PRAISE FOR THE FOUNTAIN*
> *OPENED" OLNEY HYMNS, 1779*

Mayfair, London
December 24, 1814

"*I* must admit, Mama, you were right." Nicholas tugged at his cravat, snowy white against the dark blue of his waistcoat. "She is a diamond of the first water."

"Of course she is. The betrothal benefits both families. Lady Henning and I will have beautiful grandchildren, and you will not lose your inheritance. I will never forgive your father for his recklessness, gambling away such a sum." Lady

Darby's expression hardened as she spoke of her husband, but her tone was that of a doting mother. "You are the most handsome viscount in London. What an earl you will make one day."

"Let's not wish Father away too soon. It was not *all* his fault." Nicholas took a final look at his own reflection, a mirror image of his mother's that peered back at him. They had the same burnished-gold hair and clear, light blue eyes. But the lines around her mouth had deepened, and more worry lines creased her forehead. Their gazes held for a moment and then she busied herself, brushing imaginary specks from the back of his waistcoat.

"The Duke of Colvin cheated. Granted, Father should never have staked so much on a hand of cards, but the man is a blaggard. And his son is no better, perhaps worse if the on-dits are true."

"Yes," she muttered, still avoiding his eyes. "I've heard the same. Now, it's your wedding day, and we should speak of happier times to come."

"Agreed, it's been a trying year, but I believe the darkness is behind us now." His father, the Earl of Darby, had lost an enormous amount to the blackhearted nobleman. It had been a night that still haunted his dreams. Colvin's taunting, the slow anger that had built in the earl, the vicious smug smile when that extra ace had been laid on the table. Nicholas knew the man had cheated but could not prove it. One didn't accuse a duke without proof. Even then, it would have been dangerous.

They'd had to sell most of their property to settle the debt of honor and avoid scandal, barely holding on to the estate. The debacle had taken a toll on his father's health. "You seem to have come to the rescue, Mama."

"Nonsense. Lady Henning wanted her daughter to move up in rank. As a baron's wife, this is quite a feather in their cap. Alice will be a countess when you assume the title. And we needed the dowry."

"And the lady was willing?"

"You asked her yourself, did you not?" His mother studied the evergreen garland that decorated the hearth mantel, fingering the sprigs of rosemary and ivy leaves. "What woman would not be happy for such a match? Handsome, titled husbands are hard to come by."

"I beg to disagree. *Penniless* titled husbands are more easily found, handsome or otherwise." He smirked at his mother's pursed mouth.

"I could not ask for a better Christmas celebration than having a new daughter enjoying our Yule log. I realize the banns were read rather hastily, but our family shall begin a new chapter with the New Year." She smiled up at him, her blonde hair gleaming in the sunlight that slanted through the gauzy curtains. On tiptoes, she kissed his cheek. "I must go. We leave for the church within the hour."

As Nicholas watched her leave, the image of his own children playing in front of the Yule log crossed his mind. He wanted children. Several, at least. Would they be dark like Alice or fair like himself? His stomach inexplicably tightened at the thought, and he attributed the discomfort to the approaching wedding and loss of bachelorhood.

Nicholas and his best friend from university, Gideon, the future Earl of Stanfeld, stood before St. George's, Hanover Square. The giant columns towered over them as they stood on the steps of the church. Complete opposites in looks and temperament, they had made quite a name for themselves during their time at Cambridge.

"So, did Lady Darby attach the leg shackles or was this of your own making?" Gideon grinned, his black hair shining in the morning light, deep-blue eyes twinkling with laughter. "Though I admit Miss Alice would tempt the staunchest of bachelors."

"Let's just say I don't mind making the sacrifice. And with any luck, it might turn into a love match." Nick adjusted his cravat for the tenth time since leaving the manor. "Is Pendleton coming?"

"He'll be here." Gideon slapped his friend on the back. Viscount Pendleton was the third member of their infamous university trio. "Nervous?"

"I wouldn't call it that, more a sense of foreboding." He shook his head. "I've been listening to Sarah and her fairy-tales too much of late. The Grimm Brothers have her mesmerized."

"Your sister doesn't need anything to spark her imagination." Gideon reached inside his coat and pulled out a flask. "A flash of lightning to steady the hand?"

"Gladly accepted, my friend."

"Calm yourself, Alice. I didn't mean to raise my voice." Nick smoothed back her rumpled dark hair, tipping up her chin. Deep shadows below those shimmering coffee eyes made her pale skin almost glow. She was magnificent, ebony upon ivory, docile and pliant. Or had been until he realized she'd been taken before their wedding night. While consummating their union, he found there was no barrier within her to breach.

"I was just surprised you weren't a…"

"A v-virgin."

"There is someone else? You've already given your heart to another?" A first love, an infatuation perhaps that would fade in time. He was confident enough in his own looks and lovemaking skills to overcome the first attempts of a clumsy boy.

She sniffed and shook her head, raven waves bouncing against her bare shoulders. "I can't continue this charade any longer. I am so sorry, so so sorry."

"I beg your pardon?" An icy finger of dread skittered down his spine.

She lifted a tear-stained face to him. "I am with child."

He froze, the muscles of his face paralyzed. His mouth hung open, but no words would emerge. Heat washed over him as her perfidious words sunk in. Trying to pull his thoughts together, he tied his shirtfront closed. *Hell and damnation...*

An annulment. He would get an annulment.

"I was forced."

"Raped?" He blew out a breath and ran his fingers through his hair. Had she led on a previous suitor? A flirtation gone badly? This was not how his wedding night was supposed to play out. "Who is he?"

"A nobleman's son. Mama said it would be his word against mine, that he would never be brought to justice, but I would be ruined." She grabbed his arm as he tried to stand. "Please, our mothers came up with the idea. I was against it, but I was pregnant. I—"

"Thought it would be easy enough to pass the whoreson off as my child. I was in need of funds, and you were in need of a husband." The spark of anger ignited, flames burning his stomach. What an imbecile he'd been. "Whose bloody child am I expected to raise in order to keep my estate?"

"Mama said it must be kept secret. He must never know. He's a vicious, despicable man. We don't know what he would do." Her eyes went wide with fear, those full lips he'd just kissed, trembled. "Please, don't make me tell you."

"By God, you will." Nicholas grabbed her narrow shoulders, pressing into the smooth skin, his fingertips creating red imprints in the creamy flesh. "I'll know whose by-blow I have beneath my roof."

Alice began to sob in earnest, her chest heaving as she tried to breathe, her fingers clenching his hands. "I am so sorry. So sorry..." Her head moved back and forth as she muttered her apology over and over.

He wrenched free and stormed across the room to open the window sash. He needed air; he couldn't breathe. Pressing his head against the upper windowpane, he looked out onto the dark landscape and let the chilly breeze cool the angry fire consuming him.

Alice let out a low wail, a sickening moan of pain and anguish, and clutched her belly, sinking to the floor on her knees. The light from the fire highlighted her wet cheeks and cast long, incongruous shadows off her small, delicate form. "Forgive me, please. Forgive me."

"Forgive you?" His hand curled into a fist, and he punched the wall, needles of pain searing from his knuckles through his wrist. "I am betrayed by my own mother, then my wife *on my wedding night.*" He laughed, the sound ugly and grating. "I believe I've reached my limit of absolution."

His entire body went taut as a wire. He had to get out, away from her tears, away from this hoax of a marriage. He'd been used. Nick pushed away her clinging hands as he dressed, barely registering the crimson smear his bloody knuckle left on the sleeve of her night rail.

"Don't leave me. Please, I'll make it up to you. I'll do anything," she whispered, her voice tinged with panic. "Where are you going?"

"Away. Anyplace I won't have to look at another conniving female." He yanked on his boots and threw open the door. "When I return tomorrow, we will sit down with both our *dear* mothers. By Christ, I will learn the truth."

Storming down the stairs, he bit out orders to the footman to bring round his carriage. "No, have my horse saddled instead." He needed to get away. He needed to get drunk. He needed to wipe this nightmare out of his mind.

Nicholas rode out of town, his mind whirling, cold sweat dripping down his back, his face hot with temper. Women. If his own mother betrayed him like this, how could he ever trust another female? He thought of his sister, her innocent face, and wondered if she would also grow duplicitous with age.

As he entered the outskirts of town, he squeezed his gelding's sides, sending Arthur into an easy canter and breathing in the chilly night air. The stars were bright in the black sky and twinkled merrily, mocking his mood. No snow tonight.

With a sharp kick, they galloped on, white puffy clouds trailing behind them as Nicholas left his wife and that horrid scene behind. The pounding of hooves seemed to beat in the same rhythm of the curse echoing in his mind. *Bloody hell! Bloody hell! Bloody hell!* By the time the horse tired, his anger had eased. Calmer and more rational, he turned his mount around and headed back toward the lights and noise of London.

Yes, Alice had deceived him, but she'd been as much a victim of their mothers' scheming as he had been. The poor girl had been raped, packaged off to a convenient husband, and never had the chance to look for love or even affection. Never had a say in the matter. At least he'd had a choice.

It would take time to adjust to the fact she was with child. But they had consummated the marriage, and he needed her dowry. Without it, his family would be on the rocks. His pride had been dented when he'd seen himself as hanging on Alice's sleeve, the arrangement too one-sided for his liking. But now it seemed they were even; they were using each other. So be it.

He'd deal with his mother later. For now, he'd go home to his *wife* and tell her they would come to an agreement and move on with their lives. He'd pray to God she had a girl. There was no way he would acknowledge a bastard as his heir.

Nick arrived back at the terrace house, a sleepy groom waiting on the steps to take the reins. "He needs a good cooling down. I rode him hard."

He took the stairs two at a time and threw open the door to his rooms, his chest heaving with the effort of the ride and two long flights of stairs. "Alice…" It was cold. Had the servants let the fire die?

In the sitting room of their apartment, a note lay on the table next to the door. He collected it from the silver tray, recognizing his name written in flowing letters.

Nicholas

With the envelope in hand, he entered the bedchamber. "Alice—"

An invisible iron bar hit him full force. He stumbled toward the bed, his body teetering before he sank to his knees, the letter drifting to the carpet. His eyes never left the petite body swaying from the upper rail of the four-poster bed.

Her white gown fluttered from the light breeze of the still-open window. Delicate satin slippers swung lazily before his eyes. Slowly, his gaze rose past the hand wearing his emerald wedding ring, the limp arms, to the vacant eyes of his dead wife. Her head tilted at an awkward angle, her delicate chin resting against the linen sheet tied around her long, slender neck. The once-porcelain skin he'd stroked and kissed a few hours ago, now mottled and gray.

"NOOOOOOO…" Nicholas clutched his head, rocking back and forth, cursing his wife, his mother, himself. He rose, clutched the bedcurtain, and climbed onto the mattress. Face-to-face with his dead wife, his heart clenched, the breath gone out of him. Nicholas tenderly pushed a damp tendril from her cheek. The coldness of her skin against his scraped knuckles jarred him, and he frantically began to untangle his wife from the bedclothes.

Tears blurred his vision; he cursed his trembling fingers as he tried to maintain his balance on the mattress. Finally releasing her from the linen noose, he fell to his knees and cradled her in his arms, swaying gently side to side. The door opened, and he heard a terrified gasp. He looked into his mother's horrified eyes.

"What have we done?" he whispered. "What have we done?"

CHAPTER ONE

ONCE UPON A WINDOW©

"...In as much as every discovery of what is false leads us to seek earnestly after what is true, and every fresh experience points out some form of error which we shall afterwards carefully avoid."

— JOHN KEATS

Wicked Earls' Club, London
Late October 1819

"It's just a friendly game of whist. C'mon, Darby, play with us." The marquess made another unsuccessful attempt to bring Nicholas into the game.

"I beg your pardon, my lord, but I don't indulge in gaming." Nicholas, Earl of Darby, shook his head, an easy smile curling his lips. His gaze swept the crowded room. Several men sat to his left near the fireplace, sipping drinks and engaged in conversation. Flanking the right side of the room were tables where various games of whist, faro, and hazard were in progress. "A friendly wager in the books, whether the heir will be born or a ninth daughter, perhaps whether Stanfeld will marry before he's sixty, is as far as I go."

"I'm in the books?" Gideon, the Earl of Stanfeld, scowled, his bushy dark brows coming together. "How in tarnation did I get in the books?"

"Once a man inherits an earldom, he becomes much more interesting." Nicholas laughed and slapped him on the back. "Just an example, my friend. You are not a line in the club's wagers." He chuckled. "Yet."

"I think I already regret putting you up as a member in the Earls' Club." Stanfeld tapped the golden *W* pinned to his friend's lapel. "Your standing improved, and I don't see you any closer to the parson's trap than I am."

A faded but familiar pain grazed Darby's heart, and he forced another grin. "I escaped that snare once, if you remember." He stopped a man in livery passing by. "Bring us a bottle of brandy, would you? We'll be in the billiard room." He nodded to Stanfeld and took his escape.

Nicholas made his way down the stairs, his thumb rubbing against the *W*. Wicked. Yes, he was a wicked earl and planned on keeping that title and this pin for many years. His vices did not hurt anyone nor interfere with his title or family.

Stanfeld had recommended him to the elite club. He'd had the requisite qualifications—trusted among his peers and claimed the title of earl and bachelor. The benefits included an exclusive floor of this club, a set of private rooms for each, and almost any vice for the asking. He had utilized the reserved rooms frequently. In fact, this had become a second home ever since the death of his father, a week after Nicholas's ill-fated marriage.

He had built up his reputation as a rake over the past several years, the gossips helping tremendously after his wife's death. According to the on-dits, the Earl of Darby had drowned his sorrows in alcohol when his wife had mysteriously died. Some said she had been so frightened of his wedding night demands that she had killed herself. Others spoke in whispers of possible murder, only wanting the poor chit's money and knowing that, as a peer, he could get away with it.

Neither family had ever commented or spoken of the night, much to the dismay of the prattlers who wanted the sordid details. It had taken years to quiet the tongues. But the rumors still kept nosy mothers at arm's length, worried for their innocent daughters. It kept him off the list of suitable bachelors.

In reality, the suicide had been dealt with quietly, with all the efficiency that a peer-related catastrophe was always handled. The law requiring the forfeiture of a suicide's property—in this case, dowry—was circumvented with a verdict of *non compos mentis*. A jury of his peers determined that Alice had not been of sound mind when she'd committed the deed. Alice's mother had testified to her daughter's melancholia the days before and of the wedding.

Nicholas rolled his shoulders, the expensive coat hugging his frame, and shoved that unpleasant memory away. Instead, he concentrated on the delightful redhead that would be waiting for him later in his rooms, after a mind-numbing bottle of brandy and a few games of billiards with his two closest friends. He would never repeat the mistake of his father, having no appetite for gaming. His poisons of choice were drink and the type of woman with no desire for a husband.

His present liaison was a prime article who had the misfortune to be a married to an elderly baron. The husband went to bed early in the evening, and she stayed in Nicholas's bed until early morning. They'd been meeting weekly for the past year, and it was a pleasant arrangement for both. With the confidentiality afforded by the Wicked Earls' establishment, however, his mistress could easily be whisked in and out of his rooms at the club, and no one would be the wiser. Though at times, he felt a twinge of pity for the aging baron.

Nathaniel, Viscount Pendleton, sat in a highbacked leather chair near the fire, legs crossed, head back, a glass in his hand. The embers glinted off the silver cufflink of his sleeve as he swirled an amber liquid against the cut crystal. His brown hair still held streaks of gold from the summer sun, and his green eyes were thoughtful.

"How did the brandy arrive before me? I just ordered it." Nicholas stopped at the side table and poured himself a drink from the decanter. "You seem pensive."

"I ordered a bottle of my own. I know how you hate to share, Darby," said Pendleton with a smirk. "And yes, I'm pondering a dilemma."

He sat down next to his friend, sinking into the soft leather and crossing his polished Hessians at the ankles. "Let's wait for Stanfeld, and you can tell us both at once."

"Tell me what?" The Earl of Stanfeld entered the room, followed by a man with a bottle. "Thank you, Edward." He took the decanter and set it next to the one already half-empty.

"I have a problem," said Pendleton.

Stanfeld's brows rose as he poured a drink. "A monstrous one, if the amount of alcohol is any measure."

"Ha! Nothing better than three muddled heads coming up with a solution. I'm sure we could take care of mine and solve all the world's problems with just one more bottle."

"No, that would take at least four." Nicholas stood, tossed back his last swallow, and poured another. The pleasant warmth was spreading through his body, a promise of sweet numbness and a night of dreamless sleep. He picked up a billiard stick and moved it from one hand to another, checking its weight, its straightness. "Who is the first challenger?"

Pendleton shook his head. "I'll yield to Stanfeld. You both play, and I'll talk."

As the men began their game, Pendleton told his story. "You know my sister, Hannah, was supposed to have her first season last year."

Both men murmured agreement, then with a nod from Nicholas, Stanfeld hit the first ball with a loud *crack.*

"Yes, she changed her mind about a season in London when you married Lady Eliza. Decided to get to know her new sister and wait until she was eighteen." Nicholas grinned at his opponent's miss, bent, and sent a ball into a corner pocket. "Hoping to find some sweet, handsome landowner close to home, we assumed."

Pendleton nodded. "Well, she didn't find one and was to come out this winter, arriving in Town after Eliza had the baby in late December or January. But now, Parliament has called a special session in November due to the Peterloo Massacre."

Nicholas studied the table and his next move before looking up. "Nasty business, that. Poor souls meeting at a peaceful assembly to hear a speaker, then slaughtered by their own skittish local government."

"By the by, Stanfeld, I am sorry about your cousin's death in that fiasco. I do hope your mother has recovered sufficiently?" Pendleton laid a hand on his friend's shoulder. "Bloody bad luck, that was."

Stanfeld's mouth tightened, and he nodded. "Thank you, and yes, she's doing well. His death brought about a long-postponed trip to Scotland to see Mama's ancestral home." His countenance brightened. "I almost gave in and wore a demmed kilt but knew I'd only get tangled up in the deuced thing. Now, about the Special Session. You aren't in the House of Commons, so how does it affect you?"

"It doesn't, but *you* are both members of Parliament and will be in Town..." Pendleton paused, looking uncomfortable. "Hannah wants to come for the *start* of the season. I could accompany her here, but I can't leave Eliza alone for too long."

"You *won't* leave her alone, you mean," quipped Nicholas. It was well known that Pendleton was a bit overprotective of his wife. She had been abused by a malicious father, who had tried to kidnap her while under the viscount's protection. The father had made a fatal mistake crossing Pendleton. "I haven't seen Hannah since she was a child. What kind of woman has she grown into?"

"I need you to protect her, not ogle her," said Pendleton. "Both of you."

"Won't your mother accompany her? She'd be protection enough from roving eyes." Nicholas had met the dowager viscountess once during a summer party at Pendleton Place. She had been a formidable woman. Her icy stare could a freeze a man in his tracks. "Anyway, I'm happy to be of assistance since my sister is also coming out."

"Thank you. My mother still hates coming to Town and is using the arrival of her first grandchild to avoid it." Pendleton sighed.

Stanfeld laughed. "Believe me, her daughter can be just as daunting. Hannah's a bit too assertive for my taste, but she's a tempting armful."

"She'd love to hear the tempting part." Pendleton held his glass up to Stanfeld. "You know she still sets her cap for you. I think she's convinced once you see her in London, dressed and mingling with the *ton*, you will fall at her feet and beg her forgiveness for not noticing her remarkable beauty sooner. You could even act as if you don't recognize her."

Stanfeld spit his drink out and swiped at his splattered cravat. "Good God, man, it would be like bedding my sister, and I refuse to encourage her. I, uh, have my eyes on someone."

"Oh? Did you find that bonny lass hiding in the heather while you were in Scotland?" Pendleton teased, remembering a conversation they'd had the previous summer.

The earl turned red. "As a matter of fact, I did. Mama liked Lissie so much, she brought the chit back with us. As company for her this winter, so she says."

"So she says," Pendleton and Nicholas echoed.

"Back to your dilemma. So, you want us to keep an inconspicuous eye on your sister, I assume. I'm happy to accommodate when I'm here." Stanfeld paused and took a sip of his brandy. "However, I will only attend the more pressing sessions until February. My sister is also expecting, so my mother will insist on a long visit then. Otherwise, I'll be spending more time in the country."

"So we get to meet this Scottish lass?"

Stanfeld looked embarrassed. "Truthfully, she is my cousin's widow."

"And here I thought Darby was the only scoundrel among us."

"It's not like that," Stanfeld added quickly. "They were betrothed from birth and had more of a friendship than passionate love. She's unlike any woman I've known, except Mama."

"I've heard those Scottish lasses are lively," Nicholas teased. "I look forward to meeting her."

"Back to you, Pendleton. Who will be chaperoning Hannah if not your mother?" Another *crack*, a missed shot, and a mumbled curse from Stanfeld.

"It seems Aunt Bertie has volunteered."

This time, Nicholas coughed and spluttered. Lady

Roberta was infamous in her appreciation for the male physique. Almack's had refused her entrance for a time. "I'll never forget that tabby's chubby fingers pinching my backside."

Stanfeld guffawed, mischief in his black eyes. "I heard you took the lady up on her overture."

"Devil it, I doubt I could have kept up with her, even at the tender age of twenty. I thought she finally retired to the country."

"Well, she has offered her services and is my first line of defense against the randy bachelors. You, my friends, are the cavalry she will call in if needed."

Darby climbed into the waiting hackney with his leather satchel. The driver clicked to the mare, and she pulled away with a snort, proceeding toward the outskirts of Mayfair. It was after midnight, and his man would be waiting at the Guinea.

It was a small tavern, frequented by the staff of the wealthy. Grooms and footmen relaxed at the end of a long week and complained about their masters, telling secrets about the titled families who paid their wages. He opened the canvas bag and pulled out the homespun brown jacket, frayed neckcloth, and worn boots. Removing his hat and cravat, he leaned back against the worn leather squabs and pulled off his Hessians, donning the drab attire. A few blocks from his destination, he rapped on the roof and his driver stopped. He paid the man and, with a quick word and nod, arranged for the hackney to wait.

"I should be back within the hour," Darby said as he handed him a pouch of jingling coins. He'd been using the same driver for the past year. They had come to an understanding. The hackney escorted him and kept mum; the earl paid a week's wages for a night's work.

"Aye, my lord, at yer service," the old man replied, pulling his hat down over his eyes and leaning back. "I'll be waitin' right here."

Walking the rest of the way, Darby's heels clicked along the slick cobblestones of the narrow street as he made his way toward the rendezvous point. Fog crept close to the ground, curling about his boots, obscuring the pavement then slithering away to reveal a puddle or dark outline of something he instinctively knew to sidestep. A cold mist sent a chill through him. It shrouded the buildings, lending the streets a Gothic quality that had Nicholas picking up his pace.

We're getting closer, Alice. Your death will not be in vain.

He thought of the letter, the worn paper with the fateful words she'd left him that night. Even in her turmoil, she'd known her mother was wrong. The evil that possessed the Duke of Colvin must be stopped. And so, she had told him the name of the perpetrator in her final farewell, the name of the perpetrator.

He stopped in front of the Guinea, the light spilling out onto the wet stones and illuminating two dark forms around the side of the building. Their heads were close as if in secret conversation, and a small parcel passed between them. One of the men glanced up, caught Nicholas's eye, and scurried down the alley. One of Colvin's men. Good, that's why he was here.

He entered the noisy tavern, the scent of sweat, stale beer, and cheap perfume assailing his nose. A barmaid smiled at him over her tray. He avoided her gaze and quickly moved to a back table where Walters sat with a bumper of ale. A fire blazed in a large hearth along one wall, patrons crowded around it, sharing gossip.

Some were dressed in fine clothes, displaying their prominence in a household. Others wore homespun garb, workers from the area who cleaned the streets, made deliveries to the kitchens, or performed the city's necessary menial labor. An occasional bark of laughter or shout of anger could be heard over the steady thrum of voices.

"Good evening, my lord," greeted his man with a nod as he stood. Walters waved his mug at the maid, who nodded in understanding. "Seems the duke is moving up in the world of vices."

"I saw one of his toadies outside," Darby said, sitting down at the wood table, carefully balancing himself on the wobbly stool. "Looked as if he were paying for a service."

"Indeed, sir. We'll be heading over to the Rat's Nest as soon as yer ready." His ruddy face wore a smile that didn't quite meet his brown eyes. Walters had been a Bow Street runner before working for the earl. He'd been wrongly accused of bribery when he'd come too close to solving a crime that involved a nobleman and still held a grudge toward certain aristocrats.

"St. Giles? The gin houses of Covent Garden aren't keeping him satisfied now?" Darby accepted the mug and took a long pull. "Where in this delightful rookery are we destined?"

"Seems there an interesting purchase at one of the flash houses." Walters ran thick fingers through his tangled dark brown curls, tipped with premature gray. "A house that specializes in procuring chimney sweeps."

"But Colvin isn't looking for a boy to sweep his chimney." Darby's lip curled in disgust. "Is that the transaction I witnessed outside?"

"I would assume it is." Walters winked at the barmaid as she plunked down another bumper. "Thank you, lass."

"It seems the old duke kept his son's depravity in check

while he was alive. In the past year, he's gone from gambling and elegant prostitutes to gin houses. The type known for catering to hard-to-please clients." Darby drummed his fingers on the glass and took a long pull of his ale. "He's succumbing to his dark side."

"The question is, how far will he sink? The abbess of the last place he patronized refused him entrance last week. Seems he's getting more violent and not worth the risk."

Nicholas had been watching the Duke of Colvin for the last year. A year of spies, of waiting for something that could be used against him. When Colvin's father had been alive, His Grace had kept a tight rein on his son. The previous duke had known what his heir was about and hired a bodyguard of sorts to accompany his undisciplined son. Keep him out of trouble.

Trouble. That's what the old duke had called Alice's fatal circumstances. *A troubling situation.* To date, Nicholas had witnessed several women unknowingly saved from Alice's fate as the expensive attendant had pulled his ward from a compromising scene.

In Darby's eyes, the bloody bastard *and* his father had been equally responsible for their part in Alice's death. And then there was his own role in the whole mess. So Darby, stricken with remorse, had made a vow. He would get justice for the woman who would never know love or a family of her own.

Patience. The man had been untouchable when his father had been alive. But now he was on his own, no restraining hand, not a soul to tell the wretch "no." In the past year, Colvin had lost interest in the well-born virgins. He'd gone to the gin houses instead—those known to provide for clients with *peculiar* tastes—and enjoyed some rough sport with those working women desperate enough for the coin. But his lust for inflicting pain seemed unquenchable.

Darby tossed down a shilling for the unfinished ale and stood. "Let us venture into the Rat's Nest. I have a hackney meeting us a few blocks away."

"Aye, sir. I'm in the mood to catch me a repugnant little rodent."

CHAPTER TWO

"Cheerfulness, it would appear, is a matter which depends fully as much on the state of things within, as on the state of things without and around us."

— CHARLOTTE BRONTE

Pendleton Place
Northern England
Late October 1819

*H*annah glared at the array of clothes scattered across her rooms. Nothing seemed right, and she had to look perfect. Dresses and jackets were spread across the counterpane, hanging from the bedposts, or draped over her dressing table. In the next room, petticoats, stays, and stockings were strewn over chairs and her traveling trunks. One table held shoes, slippers, and boots.

There would be walks during the day, dances, and rides in Hyde Park. It would be her first extended visit away from home. She could be in London for up to six months, except

for the trip home at Christmas and the Twelfth Night cele-
brations, which her country neighbors still practiced with
exuberance.

She fingered the pale-pink muslin with tiny roses
embroidered across the satin ribbon at the waist. The delicate flowers were repeated across the hem and cuffs. Would
it make her appear too young? Would she look a total dolt
against the backdrop of the elegant and polished *beau monde*?

Stop it! she scolded herself. Hannah was known for her
poise and self-reliance. Why should her confidence falter
over a trip to Town? Because Gideon would be there. Her
stomach did a flip, her lips curving into an instantaneous
smile. She closed her eyes, and his deep-blue gaze, raven hair,
and broad shoulders filled her vision.

Piffle! She needed to cease daydreaming about the earl. If
only she could so easily quit a habit that had become second
nature to her—since the day he'd stolen her five-year-old
heart.

"A penny for your thoughts," whispered Eliza from
behind.

She twirled around to find her sister-in-law with a hand
over her mouth, surveying the windstorm that had come
upon Hannah's rooms. "I'm selecting my clothes and having
an odious time of it. I need to look sophisticated and show
off my best features, yet young enough that I don't attract
any vile old men."

"Of course, though I don't believe that's where your mind
was just now," argued Eliza, rubbing her swelling belly. She
looked lovely in the creamy morning dress, delicately
embroidered at the cuffs and hem with a pale yellow that
matched her flaxen waves. "What do you consider to be your
greatest qualities?"

"That's the problem. They aren't visible. Intelligence, wit,
common sense—"

"Humility…" Lady Pendleton's violet eyes shone with mischief.

"Merciful heavens, I don't think I've ever been accused of that, though I only believe myself to be passable pretty." She laughed and gave Eliza a hug. "How I will miss you, sweet sister."

"You'll be home before the New Year. Perhaps even betrothed, for I don't think it will take long for someone to fall madly in love with you."

"But I only have eyes for one, and I hope this season will make him loony with jealousy and realize we are the perfect match." She sighed. "My first waltz shall be with Gideon. His strong hand on my waist, my palm against his. He will pull me close, our bodies in perfect harmony as he twirls me about the room."

"About Lord Stanfeld…" Eliza transferred a deep-green riding habit from the bed to the post and sat. She patted a space next to her, waiting for Hannah to sit before she continued. "Nathaniel has returned with news."

Hannah's brother had gone to London on some business and to arrange for the townhouse to be opened. He most likely had seen his friends. "Is Gideon in good health? Has something happened to his mother, Lady Stanfeld?"

"Everyone is fine." Eliza paused. "Do you remember when he took his mother to Scotland?"

A knot began to form in Hannah's stomach. "Yes, his cousin was killed in that political demonstration, and the Stanfelds went to offer their condolences." She didn't like the pitying expression in her sister-in-law's eyes. "He didn't marry?"

She shook her head. "No, but it seems he met someone, who Lady Stanfeld was also quite taken with, and she has returned with them."

A rock plummeted to the bottom of her belly, her chest

tightening as she stared blindly at the Axminster carpet under her feet. He'd found another? She was just coming of age, and he couldn't wait a few more months? The selfish, thoughtless scoundrel. *Horsefeathers!* Why she'd...win him over, of course. Hannah Pendleton was not one to give up easily.

"You say, he's not married?"

"No, but Nathaniel thought he sounded quite smitten." Eliza took Hannah's hand, sympathy darkening her eyes to a deep plum. "Stanfeld told your brother he plans on asking her as soon as the mourning period has passed."

"Mourning period? For a cousin?"

"The young lady is his cousin's widow."

Hannah let out a long whistle. "The proper Earl of Stanfeld wants to court the widow of his dead cousin?" She laughed then, relief untying the knot and disintegrating the rock in her stomach. "He must feel some kind of obligation toward her, and being from the Highlands, she is sure to have a certain charm. He will come to his senses."

She kissed her sister-in-law on the cheek and resumed her packing. Althea, Eliza's daughter from her first marriage, burst into the room. "Oh, the pwetty clothes," exclaimed the toddler. "Are you putting them on, Aunt Hannah? Can I watch?"

Hannah squatted down, her face level with the almost-four-year-old. "I'm so glad you've arrived. I want your opinion on each dress. Your mother and you will vote on which ones I shall pack and which shall stay behind. Can you help me?"

Althea clapped her hands, her blue-violet eyes dancing with excitement, the black curls bobbing furiously as she nodded her head. "Oh, yes! Mama lets me pick out her dwesses when she's going someplace vewy important."

Hannah gave the little girl a hug. "I'll miss you so much, Thea."

"You will be back in two blinks, Mama said." Althea returned the hug and climbed onto the bed, leaning against her mother's swollen belly. "Little Nathaniel, it's me again, your big sistah." She kissed Eliza's stomach, then settled back against her mother's swollen belly.

With the help of her audience, Hannah finished packing. It took a bit longer than expected, with Althea piping in her opinions, trying a few articles on herself, and inviting her basset hound, Cyrano, to join the party. The dog didn't seem quite as happy as his mistress after a bonnet was wrapped around his head. When he began a long, soulful howl, Eliza packed up both dog and girl and bid Hannah good night.

Sleep did not come quickly with so many plans and thoughts of Gideon in her head. She dreamt of a prince, dark and hand-some with smoldering dark blue eyes, and a princess with sepia hair and a gilded tiara sparkling with gems. They danced until she was breathless, and as he bent to kiss her, Hannah woke.

London
Early November 1819

The trip was uneventful, the weather pleasant, and the coach ride dull, dull, dull. Hannah had forgotten to pack her latest novel. Her brother, dear sweet Nathaniel, had unearthed an ancient magazine from an innkeeper's wife. She'd exhausted the pages of La Belle Assemblée. Thrice. She was now a fountain of knowledge concerning a wide variety of no-longer-pertinent subjects.

27

Masques, popular during the reign of James I, were at once a ball and an opera. *But a masquerade might be titillating,* she thought. *All those hidden faces identified only by the gleam in one's eyes or the devilish smile below the guise.* She'd found the Turkish tale of Jahia and Meimoune interesting the first read, the true story of George and Sophia better the second time, and never should have attempted the Fugitive Poetry section a third.

The humorous anecdotes of famous French women had instigated a fierce bout of yawns. She knew what performances had been seen at Covent Garden or the Cobourg Theatre and what mourning fashion had been prevalent when Queen Charlotte died this time last year.

Hannah was not accustomed to being idle. She kept busy throughout the day, either practicing the pianoforte, embroidery, painting, walking, or riding her mare. Never sitting. Just sitting. Thank goodness there was a library at the townhouse. She would remember to bring several books for the journey home. She listened to her maid's soft snore and wished *she* could sleep in the dratted rocking vehicle. She should have brought her mare and been outside with her brother, but her mother had stomped her foot and forbade it.

The coach slowed as they finally encountered city traffic. The farther into the town center, the more congested the streets. She flicked open the wooden slats and looked out at the clamor and overcrowded walkways. Parliament would assemble in another week or two, and the *ton* were gathering.

The smells of the city assaulted her nose but she breathed in deeply, anticipating the coming adventure. The curses of coachmen, chatter of those on foot, and calls of vendors all combined into a background of indiscernable nattering. The streets were still dry as the weather had been clear, and no snow had fallen yet this season.

"How do you fare, sweet sister, with two days of inactivity?" Nathaniel's question floated through the narrow openings of the window. She could see strips of his dark great coat and black riding boots as he pulled up next to her. "One magazine and two days of nothing to do but look at your lady's maid."

"Which was why she chooses to ride in the rumble seat with the footman for the last leg of the journey. She'd rather face the chill than my sour countenance." Hannah chuckled. "Not that I blame her. I think that last accidental kick from my jiggling foot did her in."

"Aunt Bertie arrived ahead of us and, according to her note, has everything in order." He winced. "I am sorry about being unable to stay and chaperone you myself. The timing couldn't be worse with Eliza."

"Don't be a ninny. I enjoy Aunt Bertie's outrageousness and am looking forward to it. Besides, I'd be disappointed in you if you weren't by Eliza's side. And Althea would be lost without at least one of us present."

"We'll have dinner with Stanfeld and Darby once we're settled in. They have been instructed to keep an eye on you and your chaperone. At least Darby's sister is also coming out, so you'll know someone before your first formal event."

"How old is Lady Matilda?" *Please don't let her be stunningly perfection.*

"Seventeen, I believe. Close to your age, of course." He grinned. "She and Lady Darby will be a voice of reason, or a shield, when Aunt Bertie makes a sham of things."

"Perhaps our aunt has matured." Hannah rolled her eyes when her brother guffawed. "I mean, in actions rather than years."

The coach rolled to a stop in front of the townhouse,

located at the end of the long brick terrace. The brick had been covered with a plaster stucco and painted a creamy pale salmon with Maritime blue door and trim.

A pair of pilasters stood on each side of the three steps leading up to the door, and to the left of the entrance, a bow window shone with a warm welcoming light. Above, miniature wrought-iron balconies graced the windows of the top three stories, which would hold baskets of flower in the summer.

The door opened and a butler appeared with a stiff bow and a bewildered expression. The look was explained as Lady Roberta pushed her ample bulk through the doorway, sending the poor man in a forward spin. Aunt Bertie grabbed his arm with her beringed fingers, her brown eyes slanted with merriment, and pulled him from almost certain mishap.

"You almost went tumbling down the stairs, Smith! Really, you should be more careful. I don't know what we'd do without you." She floated down the steps, always a remarkable sight due to her plump figure, and informed the neighborhood that they had arrived. "My lovelies," she said in a booming welcome, "I've been waiting forever and a day! Come give me a hug. It's been monstrous long since I've seen you both."

The attendant opened the door and helped Hannah from the coach. The weak streetlamp cast a golden glimmer on Aunt Bertie's face that made her appear years younger as she met Hannah at the pavement. She grabbed her niece in a tight hug before she could say a word. After an air-sucking welcome, Hannah managed, "Goodness, it is good to see you too, Aunt."

She gave her brother a sidelong glance and saw Nathaniel maintaining a polite expression while preparing himself for the forthcoming attack. Her brother had always been slightly intimidated by their independent aunt. While their father had been cordial and compliant, his sister had been full of life, pushy, and vocal in her opinions.

At seventeen, Lady Roberta had wed a wealthy baronet's second son. The father had wanted to move up in society, and Aunt Bertie had wanted his handsome son. *"It may not have been love at first sight, but it was certainly lust at first touch,"* she'd confided to those present on her niece's sixteenth birthday. It was the first time Hannah had seen her mother blush.

Lady Roberta's robust husband, however, had one major flaw. He could not swim. While on a business trip, his ship had encountered a storm and sank. The marriage contract had provided well for the widow, including a substantial jointure until she remarried or died. Finding herself plump in the pocket and independent, she shunned all future marriage proposals. At almost fifty years of age, she was still dogged by a reputation of bold flirtation and speaking her mind.

Hannah adored her Aunt Bertie. Nathaniel remained cautiously affectionate. Their mother secretly envied her.

"You must be famished. I've arranged a light repast in the parlor. I thought it would be cozier than the dining room." Lady Roberta gave orders to the footman and driver, then turned to the butler and maid. Bodies went scurrying in different directions, trunks were hauled inside, and Hannah soon found herself shed of her traveling cape and sipping a steaming cup of tea.

"You look well, Aunt," Hannah said as she filled a small plate with a chunk of cheese, sliced beef, and a thick piece of buttered bread. "And this is delicious."

Nathaniel agreed, his cheeks full as he took another bite of the meat, quickly followed by more cheese. "I didn't realize how hungry I was." He leaned back against the stuffed brocade with a sigh. "My back is stiff from so many hours in the saddle. I shall retire early tonight."

"Thank you, Hannah. I've taken to walking every day. It adds color to my cheeks, and I feel better." Patting her gray-streaked auburn bun, she continued chatting as she bit into chunk of the blue-veined Stilton. "I've also ordered cream cheese. It's monstrous good on biscuits.

The small hearth had a cheery fire, the coals burning red and orange. On the mantel were cameos of their grandparents, their father, and Roberta. Likenesses from years ago when the entire family had been alive. The Brussels carpet beneath her feet had been there since Hannah could remember.

With her toe, she traced the now-faded red floral medallions that had once brightened the room, letting memories envelop her. Her grandmother had decorated this space with vivid, warm colors and personal curiosities and portraits. Aunt Bertie refused to change anything in this room, and Hannah was happy for it.

Grandmama had insisted her grandchildren visit annually, and she and Nathaniel had stayed a week each year near St. Nicholas Day. They received gifts, always something they might have asked for throughout the course of the year. How Grandmama always knew, they never did find out. Cook would let them in the kitchen to help prepare the mince pies that would be eaten on Christmas Day. Parlor games were played every night before the fire, and an ongoing tale read to them with a special sweet treat before retiring for the night. Visits here, until the death of their grandmother, had been magical and highly anticipated.

Those weeks came to mind when she thought of her own children she would have someday. Children who would know the feel of their mother's arms around them, kisses at bedtime, and a welcome lap when they needed comforting from a fall off their pony or a dispute with a sibling. It would be her grandmother that Hannah would emulate when she was a wife and mother.

Mama loved her children, but one would not describe her as warm nor overly affectionate. Yet, she was responsible for Hannah's confidence and fearlessness in making her voice heard. She had instilled a steely graciousness in her daughter that would bide her well against the vicious tongues of the *beau monde*.

Hannah had also inherited her mother's sense of fashion and quick wit. If only Hannah knew what her father had passed on to her. Perhaps that would be a conversation with Aunt Bertie during a quiet evening spent at home.

This was one of the few places that held memories of happy family gatherings. She rose and touched the silver frames, her finger trailing along the delicately engraved metal.

"You were stunning, Aunt," she said, stopping at the likeness of Lady Roberta. "Yet you never married again."

"Pshaw! I had no desire to let another man dictate my comings and goings. My widowhood allowed me almost the same freedom as a man. I can't tell you how that irked the ladies of the *ton*. Green with envy, they were." She grinned, the dimple appearing in her left cheek. "All that whispering about my *peculiarities* and unladylike behavior was driven by jealousy. I decided at an early age, if I was to be accused of something, I may as well get some pleasure from my supposed wicked deeds."

"But did you never love anyone again? Enough to want to spend the rest of your life with him?" Hannah couldn't imagine not marrying or having children. Perhaps no one else had compared to her husband. "Or was your husband your true love?"

"He was my first love," she said wistfully, her brown eyes

softening. "But not true love. He... I... Well, that's a story for another day."

"He was a handsome man, my brother, wasn't he?" Aunt Bertie changed the subject, picking up another frame. "I still miss him every day. You have his best traits, Nathaniel. The golden-brown hair and tawny eyes, his athletic nature and generosity of spirit."

"And I never knew him." Hannah had heard the stories, of course, and had listened to countless comments from her mother and aunt. Her mother had never been reticent in her disdain for her husband. Her aunt had never believed the rumors of her brother's infidelities. Nathaniel rarely spoke on the subject at all. "I wish I'd had the chance." *To make up my own mind on his character or lack of.*

"He was a good man, regardless of the on-dits at the time," her aunt consoled. "Just not strong enough for this world *or* your mother. A gentle soul who was never meant to shoulder such heavy responsibility. If my eldest brother had survived, *he* would have been perfect for Lady Pendleton. Proper, rigid—"

Nathaniel cleared his throat, indicating his unease with the direction the conversation had taken.

She ignored him and continued speaking to Hannah. "You are at an age now where we should have a long talk about the past. *Before* we attend any public functions."

"For tonight, let us be glad to be together again. What a splendid season it shall be, eh?" Nathaniel's voice lifted in false enthusiasm, and both women recognized it.

"Lud! Do not fret, nephew, I will not slight your mother," she relented. "Now, how was the trip? Uneventful, I hope."

"I don't think you've ever hoped for that," mumbled Nathaniel.

"Dull. I forgot to bring a book and thought I would go

mad." Hannah whispered loudly, "I have taken to novels as of late."

"And with that tidbit of information, I shall take my leave."

She watched her brother depart, then turned her attention to a shelf with glass and ivory figurines. She picked up a tiny china bell and smiled at the clear, light *tinkle*.

"Your father bought that for Mama before he went off to university. I swear that woman kept everything." A thoughtful expression crossed her still lovely face. "She was a sentimental soul. She passed that tenderness on to her son and the good sense to me. Another reason I never married again."

"You don't approve of marriage?"

"Of course I do! Marriage is a wonderful institution for some. I tried it, enjoyed it, and moved on to the next adventure."

"So, no regrets?"

"Ah, that's a tricky question. One always has regrets. More to the point, would I do it the same way again?" Aunt Bertie nodded, her dimple deepening. "Without a doubt."

CHAPTER THREE

"Never will I give my hand where my heart does not accompany it."

— ANN RADCLIFFE

"*I* left my card at Darby's townhouse," Nathaniel informed the ladies next morning at breakfast. "I went for an early ride, before Rotten Row was crowded, and stopped by on my way back."

"And Lord Stanfeld?" asked Hannah. She'd prefer to see Gideon first.

"He won't be back to Town until the session begins. He's been busy at home with his mother and *company*. Perhaps you should focus your attention elsewhere." His tone was insistent and meant to put his sister off.

"Oh, piffle! He's not even betrothed. If I ever believe him to be in love with another, then I'll sample the other pies." She giggled at the horrified look on her brother's face.

"She didn't get that from me. I did not tell her anything about *wares* and sampling." Lady Roberta defended herself. "I only mentioned that testing the waters can be a wise thing. One never knows what sort of man is compatible until one has met that particular type."

Nathaniel opened his mouth, closed it, then took a sip of his coffee. "I think I already need something stronger added to this. Fortification for the day."

"What is the schedule for today, nephew?" She rubbed her hands together. "I so enjoy meeting new people."

"As I said, I've left my card at Darby's, so he's first on the list. I'm hoping his mother can get vouchers to Almack's."

"Oh, yes, Mother said I must be seen there." Hannah slathered the thick cream cheese on her bread and sank her teeth into it. Sooo good. Talking around her mouthful, she asked, "Aunt Bertie, you can't inquire about Almack's?"

Silence. The only sound was Hannah chewing her bread and cheese. Then both Aunt Bertie and Nathaniel burst out in loud guffaws.

"Oh, my dear, you are a cake. While I was only denied a voucher for a short time, my influence has still not improved." She bit her bottom lip, the laugh lines around her brown eyes deepening as she chuckled. "I raised a bit of a breeze there when I was younger. If those walls could whisper, there'd be some ears pressed against them."

"It seems there is much I don't know about London and my own aunt." Hannah put her nose up. "I expect to be educated on all of your stories before the end of the season."

"My pleasure, sweet niece," agreed her aunt.

"This may be the longest week of my life," groaned Nathaniel. He stood and wiped a few crumbs from his olive-green waistcoat. The buckskin breeches had a coffee stain on the right leg, and he cursed softly as he tried to wipe it off with his napkin. "Dash it all! Now I'll have to change."

"Such a fuss over nothing." Hannah waved a finger at him. "We have to change clothes sometimes three times a day, so don't expect any sympathy from us."

"I think he misses his wife and pretty little stepdaughter," added Aunt Bertie.

With a snort, Nathaniel tossed the napkin back on the table. "We will depart by three o'clock. I'll have the carriage brought round, so please be ready." He managed a stern glare at Hannah. "I mean it, promptly at three."

"Of course, I'm always punctual."

Aunt Bertie and Nathaniel shared another look, another burst of laughter.

"Well, I try anyway," she admitted with a pout.

"We leave in quarter of an hour, dear," announced Aunt Bertie from the other side of the room. "Do *not* give your brother reason to gloat."

Hannah smoothed out the pale-rose skirt. The white cotton walking dress had a modest neckline with puce Vandyke points of lace that repeated in a double row at the calf and again along the hem. A satin ribbon matching the lace adorned the waist, with a redingote of the same color over the dress. The double layer of petticoats would keep her warm in the chilly November temperatures, along with her gloves. Now for her hair.

Her maid fretted behind her, a silver brush in one hand and combs in the other. "Please, Miss, we don't have much time."

Hannah sat down with a sigh and gazed at the mirror. Her dark honey-colored waves hung loose down her back. Within ten minutes, the efficient lady's maid had swept her mistress's hair up into a loose chignon, attached a ribbon matching the one on her dress, and pulled out curls to frame her face. Wrapping two longer strands from the back around the curling tongs, she laid each warm curl over Hannah's shoulders.

Another rap at the door, and then Aunt Bertie entered. "Pish and a pox on you, girl, if you aren't ready. We must get down those stairs now." Her aunt stood, clutching her gray embroidered reticule, a slate redingote over her pale-lavender day dress. She patted her own simple chignon, pulled back with only a few curls in front of her ears. "I hate that smug look Nathaniel wears every time you are late."

"I'm well aware of my brother's condescending looks," she said, thanking her maid quietly and pulling on her gloves. "Are we ready for our next adventure?"

"Indeed!"

They'd just arrived in the entrance hall when Nathaniel appeared from the drawing room.

"Well, I'll be hornswoggled." Her brother gave a low whistle, surprise in his eyes as he and the footman helped them on with their wool pelisses. He donned his greatcoat over fawn-colored breeches and gleaming Hessians. Placing the beaver hat over his burnt umber curls, he added, "Either you are excited to meet the acquaintance of your first London friend, or Aunt Bertie is a good influence on you." He held out both arms to escort the ladies to their conveyance as the butler held open the entrance door. "You both look lovely, by the way."

"I believe it's a bit of both," answered Hannah as they descended the few steps and walked between the wrought-iron fence to the pavement. "You know how competitive Aunt is, and she hates anyone having a leg up on her."

The gleaming black carriage, with the Pendleton crest of gold on the side, was led by a pair of matching bays snorting white puffs into the chilly afternoon air. It seemed a busy time of day, for two town coaches and barouche stood ready along the terrace. Settling back against the cushioned squabs, Hannah smiled. It was a lovely day. The sun shone, and the green topiaries behind the iron fences seemed to beckon to her as the carriage lurched forward and into the traffic.

She gripped the leather strap and bent forward, looking at the houses they passed, marveling at the size of some of the structures. Her aunt provided a steady stream of commentary of who lived where, who had previously rented and who now occupied a residence, along with other interesting tidbits about the personages of Mayfair. They left the neighborhood of Berkeley and soon entered Hanover Square, passing by St. George's.

The driver called to the horses and they slowed, approaching a crescent of townhouses made of a pale-yellow limestone. Nathaniel led them up to a deep red entrance door, flanked by pillars and a carved pineapple above the threshold. Bow windows graced each side, and Hannah marveled at the size of the entrance hall.

Their heels clicked on the polished marble floor as they were led into the drawing room by a stiff butler. The drawing room was large and square with dark paneled walls, heavy velvet drapes pulled back to allow the sunlight to fill the room. Overstuffed chairs were clustered around the room, with the largest group facing an intricately embroidered chaise longue. The Axminster carpet was thick and plush beneath their feet, and the entire room bespoke wealth.

A petite young girl sat in a huge leather chair by the fireplace, a book open in her lap. She quickly closed the cover and stood to greet them, pulling down the skirt of her yellow primrose muslin as she rose. Behind them a deep voice instructed the butler.

"We will expect tea within the half hour. Lady Darby will

not be attending us this afternoon. She has the megrim and is requesting chamomile tea in her room."

His deep timbre sent a warmth rushing through Hannah. As she turned to meet their host, she caught his eye and he smiled. Her breath caught.

"Pendleton, it's good to see you!"

"And you," said Nathaniel, as he leaned forward and shook his friend's hand. "I'd like you to meet my sister, Miss Hannah Pendleton, and I believe you met my Lady Roberta before?"

Aunt Bertie elbowed Hannah, reminding her to breathe as her aunt put her hand forward and nodded in acknowledgment of the introduction. Darby bowed over each lady's gloved hand.

"My pleasure," he said, lifting his translucent calamine-blue eyes to Hannah. He had waves of sun-gold hair that shone even in the dim room. "And may I introduce my sister, Lady Matilda."

When Matilda joined them, Hannah had to pull her gaze from his, mesmerized by the odd translucent shade of a clear summer sky.

"It is a pleasure to meet any friends of my brother." Her voice was soft, neither shy nor confident. Matilda pushed a blonde lock, the shade of evening primrose, from her forehead. "I apologize for my mother's absence." She gripped her book, her white knuckles betraying her calm tone.

Hannah's heart went out to the girl. "Is that by Maria Edgeworth? Have you read many of her books? I so enjoyed her novel, *Leanora*."

A grateful smile curled the girl's lips. "Oh, yes. That's why I purchased *Castle Rackrent*. Have you read it?"

"No, I haven't. Perhaps I could borrow it when you finish?"

"Oh, yes. Do you read any biographies?"

"Egad! Please don't tell me we have two bluestockings on our hands," Nathaniel said with a laugh.

"My sister has her nose in a book most of the time." Darby grinned, the dimple in his cheek deepening. "She's indiscriminate and will read anything from a scientific journal to a romantic novel."

Hannah's eyes snapped back to the earl's face. She had the strangest urge to step closer, reach up, and trace her finger along the cleft in his chin. Wings had taken flight in her belly. *What was happening?* While Gideon had always sent her stomach into a tumble, she'd never experienced a flock of birds flapping inside her.

It must be exhaustion from the trip. Or those captivating eyes. Or the dimple that begged her to press her lips to his cheek. Or the stretch of his jacket across those broad shoulders and the thigh-hugging buckskin breeches. *Stop being a buffleheaded romantic,* she scolded herself.

Aunt Bertie looked at Hannah, then gave Darby an appreciative perusal. "Lud! This will be a delicious season. Let's sit down and get to know one another, shall we?"

Nicholas opened the shutter and saw the guests arriving. "Another one of your sudden megrims? How convenient." Dealing with his mother always put him in a dudgeon. "These agues always seem to come upon you whenever you are avoiding a situation."

"Please give Lady Pendleton and her daughter my regards, and I hope to see them at another engagement," replied an unaffected Lady Darby, tugging the nightcap firmly over her graying chignon, her light blue eyes narrowed. "I'm certain I will recover soon. Please remember this was your idea, not mine."

"I beg your pardon?" He turned from the window and strode to the bed. "You want me to tag along during Mattie's come-out, enduring the rounds of social events, so I can point out the rakes that I've come across."

"You would know of any secrets the young men hide better than most, with the circles you frequent." She held his glare. "I don't want any surprises once Matilda is betrothed."

"Yes," he agreed, laying his fists on the mattress and leaning close to his mother. "We both know how that can spoil one's wedding night."

"I have apologized for five years. Short of announcing my part in the plot at court or shouting it from the rooftop of St. Paul's, I cannot express my regret any more than I have." She lifted her chin, an air of authority coming over her. "Now, please go down and see to your guests."

He didn't budge. "What I'd like to know is why you are avoiding Pendleton?"

"I'm not. It's his mother I'm not quite ready to face." She picked at a thread on the counterpane. "I was quite…active with the on-dits following her husband's death. I'm not proud of it, but I was jealous."

"Jealous of Lady Pendleton?" This was a new revelation coming from his tight-lipped mother. Perhaps she *was* ill. "For what reason?"

She hesitated then blew out a long breath. "I was young and fancied myself in love with the viscount—before he inherited the title. We all thought she would marry the older brother but then he was killed in that terrible carriage accident. It was before I'd met the earl, of course."

Nicholas sat down, dumbfounded. "You held a torch for Nathaniel's father?"

His mother remained silent, a sullen look turning down the corners of her mouth. "I had convinced myself that she was his ruin and didn't love him. With me, he would have remained faithful and not been caught in the marquess' bed."

"So a decade later, you attain revenge from a horrified widow, in the midst of a scandal, to soothe your vanity?"

"I said I wasn't proud of it, but I watched the joy fade from his eyes the longer he was married to her," she mumbled with a sniff. "She drove him into another woman's bed, a married woman, mind you, and then loudly proclaimed her scorn for him to save her own reputation. She shamed him into going through with the duel, knowing he was a terrible marksman."

"You branded her as a devil's daughter?" Nicholas was flabbergasted. He'd heard the malicious gossip of Pendleton's cuckolding. Women never ceased to amaze him. Their minds were more devious than most men could even imagine. "Tell me, did muddying her name make your grief more bearable?"

"No, as I said, I regret my part in that scandal."

"And what did *your husband* do through all your pining?"

"Do not be callous, Nicholas. You know I cared deeply for your father."

He snorted. "Well, you'll be pleased to hear Lady Pendleton did not come to Town. It seems she fears the *ton* has a long memory and doesn't want any whispering to over-shadow her daughter." He went to the door. "I'll expect you to be civil to her replacement, Lady Roberta."

Nicholas smiled as he heard the gasp behind him. That should be good retribution.

Entering the drawing room, he saw Pendleton standing with two women. Mattie had risen and approached the group. He turned to the butler hovering outside the thick pocket doors. "We will expect tea within the half hour. Lady Darby will not be attending us this afternoon. She has the megrim and is requesting chamomile tea in her room."

He moved into the room, observing the profile of a woman with dark toffee-colored ringlets falling down the back of a slender neck. She was exactly the type of woman he usually chose for a mistress. Not too fair, not too dark, an ample bosom, rounded hips, curves in the right places without being overly plump. He tamped down the desire that had flared and decided not to postpone the tryst with his mistress.

The lady turned to face him, and his heart skipped a beat. Eyes that matched her hair, a deep golden brown with gilded flecks, caught his and held him rooted to the spot.

He held out a hand. "Pendleton, it's good to see you."

Introductions were made, and he avoided Lady Roberta's keen gaze like an embarrassed schoolboy. Focusing on Miss Pendleton, he murmured, "My pleasure," and heard the intake of breath as he took her fingers in his and bowed over her hand. A jolt ran through him, but when he looked up she was studying him intently. He had the impression she wanted to lean in closer, an almost imperceptible movement of her body. A strange sense of loss washed over him when she did not.

"And may I introduce my sister, Lady Matilda," he said in return. The conversation became a hum in the background as he watched her make Mattie's acquaintance.

She made a comment on the book Mattie held, and Nicholas saw the kindness in Miss Pendleton's eyes. They discussed titles and authors, and his sister visibly relaxed, her shoulders easing and hands moving as she spoke. So his friend's sister was as lovely in spirit as in the flesh. He hadn't known if the girl would take after the cold viscountess or her brother, but her countenance was warm and inviting. And a fetching little morsel, which is why Pendleton had warned him off. The words *two bluestockings* invaded his brain, and he struggled to enter the conversation again.

"My sister has her nose in a book most of the time. She's indiscriminate and will read anything from a scientific journal to a romantic novel." His words directed Miss Pendleton's attention back to him.

Those eyes, the color of creamed chocolate, held him captive. Humor and intelligence, rather than shrewdness, twinkled in them. She seemed...genuine. When he flashed a smile, the pink of her cheeks made heat rush through him. *Damme, but she's a lovely chit.*

He felt another's eyes on him and turned to find Lady Roberta contemplating both of them, a knowing grin on her face. *By Christ, that woman misses nothing!*

"Lud! This will be a delicious season," said the matron. "Let's sit down and get to know one another, shall we?"

As Mattie served tea, they discussed upcoming public events and invitations that might be received in the future. Lady Roberta was in London often and kept in touch with many of those who enjoyed entertaining, listing those from who she expected to receive calls and invites. "We will, of course, have several dinner parties at our townhouse." She took a sip of tea and added more cream. "I assume Lady Darby will also be arranging teas or possibly a ball? Your home is larger than ours, and I've seen the size of the ballroom upstairs."

"My mother spoke of planning a monthly event. I believe a tea for November, a dinner for December, and perhaps a ball in January." Mattie offered the plate of small, crustless sandwiches and biscuits. "I must admit my nerves are getting the better of me, though Darby assures me I will blend in with the others."

"Why would you want to do that?" asked Miss Pendleton. "I cannot wait for my first waltz. I've only been able to practice with my brother"—she gave Nathaniel an apologetic look—"and I can only imagine what it's like..."

Her voice drifted off as she focused on choosing a treat from the plate. Nicholas's smile widened at her easy distraction. She nibbled at a delicate *fairy* cake, her tongue darting out to catch the butter icing at the corner of her mouth. He stifled a groan and struggled for conversation to change the direction his mind was taking.

"I would be honored to be your first waltz, Miss Pendleton," he said, surprising himself and receiving a pair of narrowed green eyes glaring at him. *Bloody hell*, he thought as his smile faltered, *this chit could get me into trouble.*

The lady froze in midbite at his words, as if the last thing she had intended was for him to request a dance. She finished chewing and then cleared her throat. "That would be nice, indeed, Lord Darby."

Her tone confounded him. Nicholas was not used to a lady turning him down. While he was known as a rake, he was handsome and titled. He had learned how to use a smile, a tone, or a look to get what he wanted, when he wanted it.

"I am accomplished in the waltz," he assured her. "I will not step on your toes or allow any mishaps." He tilted his head and raised one brow, knowing the hole in his cheek sank deeper. He saw the blush creep to her cheeks and his confidence returned.

Lady Roberta flipped open her fan, her wrist moving back and forth rapidly. "Merciful heavens," she gushed, "this will be a monstrous good time."

CHAPTER FOUR

ONCE UPON A WIDOW©

"Alas, that love, so gentle in his view, should be so tyrannous and rough in proof."

— WILLIAM SHAKESPEARE, *ROMEO AND JULIET*

London
Mid-November 1819

The last week had been everything Hannah had hoped for; the only thing missing was Gideon. Her brother had been a grand host, escorting her and Aunt Bertie to Hyde Park when the weather allowed, a dinner party with a baron and another with the second son of a duke. Mercy, but she didn't know how her aunt remembered all the names.

They had visited Gunther's and ate ices, despite the temperatures outside. Lady Roberta introduced her to the decadent pleasure of ice cream and hot chocolate together. Cold then hot, cold then hot. Her mouth watered thinking of it.

She also took Hannah shopping along Oxford and Bond Street, unable to do without a pair of new gloves at Wedgwood's and a variety of costly teas at Twinings. Hannah was already privy to her aunt's satinwood tea caddy. The locked box had an ebony line inlay with two compartments that held an exotic variety of tea leaves and a glass mixing bowl in the center.

"Next week, we'll stop at Grafton's. I need additional trimmings for my new bonnet. It's a bit plain," mused her aunt as they sat in the parlor, sipping a cup of tea to warm them from their recent walk in the garden.

"Why did you not choose another if it wasn't to your taste?" Hannah wondered aloud.

"Oh, I'm never quite satisfied with purchases or recipes. I always have to add or take something away."

"Recipes? You are familiar in a kitchen?" She was always learning something new about this unconventional woman.

"My traveling has made me more self-sufficient than most women of my status. I tend to wander off to the less congested areas when I visit a country. Attach myself to some unknowing local so I see how the inhabitants live, not what the privileged want us to see. The sights, the smells, the sounds of foreign places hold such delight for me. I've learned I don't need to depend on others."

"Except your father-in-law's solicitor," Hannah countered with a smirk.

"Oh no, dear. I've made wise investments over the years, some with the help of your brother. If my widow's jointure were to disappear tomorrow, I'd still be quite comfortable. I have my own solicitor for the rest of my funds, so that family really has no strings attached to me." She said it with pride in her voice. "I was quite proud to be able to help your brother hold on to certain properties after your father died."

"This townhouse for one. You realize he considers it

more your property than his." Hannah had come to realize that Aunt Bertie was not quite the buffleheaded woman many considered her to be.

While she was often impulsive in her social interactions, her words not always coming out with the correctness expected, Lady Roberta was clever with a quick wit. From the small gatherings and conversations this week, her aunt had displayed knowledge on a wide variety of subjects. Despite her eccentricities, Hannah found herself wanting to be more like Aunt Bertie.

But with a husband. Whose name was Gideon, Earl of Stanfeld.

"Aunt, did you never find a gentleman who would allow you to...be you?" She wasn't sure why it bothered her that Aunt Bertie was alone, but it did. "Are you never lonely?"

"Lonely?"

"Yes, without a—a man."

"Oh, gracious, you know better than that." She chuckled. "I think you mean, specifically, a husband?" she asked with a raised brow.

Hannah nodded.

"At times, I get lonely. But many women my age are also widowed and alone. And to answer your first question, yes, several gentlemen."

"That would not have tried to conform you?" Another surprise.

"Don't look so astounded! I've been proposed to even past the age of thirty, men promising to give me free rein. They were either smitten and too malleable for my taste or had not a feather to fly with." She leaned back, a faraway look in her eye. "But I refused to marry without sincere affection on both sides."

"You never fell in love again?"

"Oh, I never said that." Aunt Bertie busied herself with pouring more tea, an uncharacteristic look on her face.

Was that embarrassment? It couldn't be. "You were in love, then, and it was not returned?"

Her aunt let out a long sigh. "I have not spoken of him in years."

"Oh, please share," begged Hannah. "Unless it's too painful." Perhaps it was unrequited love and better left buried.

"He was the third son of a marquess. I was almost thirty-three at the time. I was travelling in India, and he was in military service. Oh, how dashing he looked in uniform…" Her voice faded away, memories taking her from her recitation.

Hannah waited patiently and nibbled at a biscuit. She studied the frames on the mantel, picturing her aunt as a young woman, vibrant and flirtatious.

"He was quiet, reserved, and oh, so handsome. Broad shoulders, chestnut hair, and soft brown eyes that made you feel welcome and safe." She paused and turned an emerald ring on her finger over and over. "I think I fell in love the moment I saw him. He said it was the first dance for him. It was so romantic, but then again, everything in India was so romantic."

"What happened?"

"We came back to England. He had a small retainer and some land and wanted to be a country gentleman." She smiled. "I wanted to travel and see more of the world."

"Did he want to marry?"

"Oh, yes. He even insisted children were not of importance due to my age. There were plenty in his family, and he was not responsible for producing an heir. He was willing to compromise and spend half his time in England and the other half traveling with me." She shook her head. "I considered it until I visited his estate. It was where he belonged, where he would be happiest. Chester was not an adventurer, he loved having a home and constancy."

"Did he not try to convince you?" Hannah reached out and grasped her aunt's hand. This was better than a novel.

"Oh, yes. For an entire year. I was too afraid he would be unhappy or come to regret my corky tendencies. We were such opposites, and I had created an image of him in my head that I couldn't change." Aunt Bertie smiled, her eyes shining. "But in truth, I think I was too frightened to trust him, to believe that a man would give up so much for me. I preferred seeing him as a romantic figure, the dashing soldier in India, rather than chance his love fading."

"Have you never seen him again?" Hannah was fascinated by this romance.

She shook her head. "I'll tell you a secret I've never shared with another soul. Chester is my only regret. I saw him as a country squire, and I'll never know if he might have been happy with me. If I might have been happy…"

"Why don't you try to find him?"

"I kept news on him for several years, read of his marriage and the birth of two children. It comforted me to know that, and I let him go." She stood abruptly. "It's still a beautiful day. Let's go for a ride, and see who is all the crack at Hyde Park, shall we?"

Aunt Bertie's confession stayed with Hannah. People were not always what they seemed. It could be terrible sin against a person to set one's mind against them because of what they appeared to be. Society had an image of Lady Roberta that did not do her justice. Her aunt had maintained an image of her true love that she'd been afraid to examine too closely.

She dressed for bed, and as her maid plaited her hair,

Hannah's mind drifted to her sister-in-law. Eliza had been terribly abused by her father, married off to a rich earl, who died within a year, and left pregnant. When Hannah had first met her and her young daughter, Althea, she'd considered the widow timid and shy. The countess would flinch if someone raised their hand too quickly. A weak woman who had no more spirit or courage than a mouse.

Yet when Eliza had been confronted with evil, first a highwayman and then her own father, she'd shown a valor that would make a soldier proud. Her sister-in-law carried a strength hidden deep inside, coming out only when needed, but it was there. Hannah had realized then the mistake she might have made by judging the woman too quickly. It was a good lesson to remember as she was introduced in London. A first impression may not always be the correct impression.

The next morning, their little family gathered in the dining room for breakfast.

"Did I mention Lady Matilda and Lord Darby will be joining us tonight for dinner? It's Nathaniel's last night, so I thought it would be a nice sending off." Aunt Bertie dropped a lump of sugar into her tea and stirred. "I will miss you, dear nephew."

"As will I," agreed Hannah, "but I am pleased I've made a few friends before your departure. Lady Matilda and I have grown quite close in such a short time."

"It grieves me to leave such beautiful ladies, but I have more females seeking my attention at home." He set a full plate of eggs, rasher, and toast on the table and gave a gallant bow. "A man's duty and all that."

"Pish! We will still have Darby to attend to us," Aunt Bertie added with a smirk at Hannah. "I believe the gentleman likes you as well as his sister does. I catch him staring at you often."

"Me? No, he must be observing Mattie. He seems very protective over her, don't you think?"

"Yes, but it's more than that."

Nathaniel's fork clattered against his plate. "I don't believe he would be a suitable match for Hannah, so please do not encourage it, Aunt Bertie."

"Why ever not?" Her brown eyes narrowed, displeasure bringing down the corners of her mouth. "I thought he was a good friend of yours."

"He is. But his reputation as a rake is not all unfounded. And he has no desire for leg shackles." Nathaniel attacked his food with vigor, dismissing the subject. "Do you ladies have any appointments today?"

"Excuse me, but let's go back to Darby. He's a rake?" Hannah had not been privy to much of the gossip yet. It was hard to believe of Mattie's brother. He seemed so thoughtful and jovial.

"Does he gamble?"

"No, he never gambles. His father almost lost their entire fortune due to some large stakes with a corrupt duke. The scoundrel had cheated, but no one could prove it. As a gentleman, Darby's father was obligated to make good on the note."

"Ah yes, the infamous debt of honor," Aunt Bertie said with an indelicate snort. "Even to a cheat."

"As I said, no one could prove it." He shook his head. "It was the reason for his ill-fated betrothal."

"I heard rumors about his brief marriage." Their aunt clucked her tongue. "Poor thing, dying on her wedding night."

"On the wedding night!" Hannah gasped. "I knew he was a widower, but I didn't realize... Oh my, what happened?"

"The on-dits at the time claimed she committed suicide, she *hung* herself." Aunt Bertie shuddered. "There was more to it than that, I'm sure."

"Well, I don't want this to be repeated because Darby is a very private man, despite his cheery countenance." Nathaniel leaned forward, pinning Hannah with his gaze. "I know how tongues wag, and since he is a friend and you are becoming close with his sister, I will tell you the truth."

Hannah put down her tea. "Continue, please."

"It seems the late Lady Darby was with child when she consented to the betrothal. In fact, her mother and Darby's mother were confidantes and came up with the scheme. One needed a father for the child, the other needed money to replenish the funds lost by the aforementioned gambling disaster."

He paused to smear creamy butter over his bread and took a bite while his sister took in this revelation. "He discovered part of the deception on the wedding night, when she was not a, er... Well, you know. When confronted, she admitted to the plot. He was enraged, and rightly so, but he stormed out of the room when she would not identify the father's name. We assume the guilt consumed her, and she ended her life that night."

"How tragic," exclaimed Hannah.

"As you might guess, he tends not to trust the opposite sex. His sister is the exception, and I believe that is due to her innocence." He waggled the butter knife at Hannah. "Don't get any ideas about saving a poor, heartbroken wretch. When he does finally marry, it will be for the purpose of producing an heir. He has no faith in love or the fidelity of women. You, my *dear* sister, deserve better than that."

"I won't argue with you, *dear* brother," she mimicked. "As you know, I have my cap set for someone else. He couldn't be more opposite than the unfortunate Darby.

"I told you, he—" Nathaniel groaned. "Good God, I give up. Aunt Bertie, my condolences to you throughout the next months, and may I wish you the best of luck?"

"Oh, my boy," she said with a wicked glint in her soft brown eyes, "luck will have nothing to do with it."

CHAPTER FIVE

ONCE UPON A WIDOW©

"If music be the food of love, play on."

— WILLIAM SHAKESPEARE

December 1, 1819

"Thank you again, Nicholas, for escorting me tonight." Matilda pulled her hand from the fur-lined muff and placed it on her brother's arm. "It's nice to have a friend my age. Hannah is so easy to talk to, and I can get so tongue-tied."

"I'm glad you both get along so well. I like her too." He patted her hand. "It's the least I can do for my doting sister."

Matilda was a thoughtful quiet girl. Her pale hair and luminous blue eyes gave her a fragile appearance, but he sensed an inner strength in her that she hadn't realized herself yet. Still, he tended to be overprotective.

She was the only female in the realm that he trusted, and her innocence was to be guarded. While he was the first to admit she had been sheltered, he'd never concede to his mother that he'd planned on staying by Mattie's side throughout the season. Regardless of his loathing for the plotting mamas and simpering daughters he'd have to face.

A smile or pleasant word came easily to his lips, and most women succumbed to his lethal combination of charming rogue. The type of man they should avoid, a splendid fellow by appearance but smoky, hiding a dark side only whispered about. He encouraged the opinion that he was a bang-up cove—dashing, good-natured, plump in the pocket, but determined to remain a bachelor. His male peers saw a different side.

By his mere presence, dandies of a certain character would steer clear of Mattie, not wanting to risk the wrath of the dubious Earl of Darby. Any man facing him in the ring at Jackson's Saloon recognized the dark determination in his eyes. He was known to have *bottom*, able to endure a beating and wait for the moment to plant a facer or finish off his opponent with a blow to the gut. That contrast of character was what made him dangerous and kept men wary.

He politely spurned attempts at further friendship and was considered unpredictable since few men knew him well. Darby was smiling and sharing a bottle with a group of aristocrats one night and a bruiser in the boxing ring the next. He preferred the solitude, having more important business to attend to. Besides Pendleton and Stanfeld, the only man he confided in was Walters. And the ex-Bow Street runner was the only person who knew of his incognito forays into the rookeries. The less society knew about his activities, the better.

The coach stopped in front of the fashionable townhouse near Berkeley Square. Lamps were lit along the street and on each side of the gate leading into the house. They were met at the door by the butler, the voice of Lady Roberta boomed from the drawing room on the right.

"Smith, did you procure a wooden plate? And the feather? Oh never mind, I've plenty of feathers." A brief pause. "But we will need the plate."

The butler tried valiantly to wipe the martyred look from his wizened face but failed. In a tired but placating tone, he answered, "Yes, my lady, I have secured the plate and two ostrich feathers, one large and one small." With an apologetic smile, he announced the guests. "Lord Darby and Lady Matilda."

Hannah hurried across the room to meet them, clasping both of Mattie's hands in hers. "It's December already, can you believe it? I feel as if we've been friends for years." She blushed. "Well, months anyway."

Her gaze moved away from his sister and her golden-brown eyes held his. The attraction he tried to pretend was nonexistent hit him again full force. "Miss Pendleton, it is a pleasure to see you again," he greeted with a bow over his hand. The scent of apricot settled on him as he kissed her gloved knuckles, his lips lingering as the warmth bombarded his innards.

Fiend seize it! Those full lips, curling up into such a smile, had made him daring. Each event, each house party seemed to increase his reaction to her.

Her evening dress of Pomona green, with deep-gold ribbons that matched the honey streaks in her hair, hugged her curves as she moved into a slight curtsy. "My lord."

Lady Roberta descended upon them. "Welcome. We have a delicious menu planned, and I've selected some enter-taining parlor games for later." She held out her hand to Nicholas with an impish grin and said, "Please don't be uncomfortable because of my past indiscretions. I promise to keep my hands to myself. I'm quite the matron these days."

That created a round of guffaws. It put Darby at ease, and

he responded good-naturedly, "I somehow doubt that term will ever apply to you, my lady."

After two glasses of claret and Lady Roberta's lively regale of her adventures in the West Indies, they entered the dining room. Since the party was not large, a smaller table had been set up for a more intimate meal. He found himself next to Miss Pendleton with his sister seated across from them. He poured wine for both of them while he deliberated on the next topic of conversation.

"Are you enjoying London, Miss Pendleton, or are you missing the country?" He turned to give her his full attention, ignoring the glare from her brother. Dash it all, he was only conversing with her. And the devil, how the wine had gone to his head.

"I am enjoying myself immensely. There is so much to see, so many family names I've heard of that I am able to put a face to."

Her hand touched his forearm and he almost laid his own palm on top without thinking. The candlelight reflected chips of gold in her eyes as she spoke, and he found himself praying no one else would speak to him. He couldn't pull his gaze from her. "Where have you been since we last met? Who have you met?"

As she spoke, he studied her face. The flawless ivory skin, the pert nose with a dash of freckles across the top, the glorious brown waves, and the hollow at her throat that begged for a kiss.

"Lord Darby? Did you say you knew them? Lord Falsen and his wife?" Miss Pendleton waved a hand in front of his face and gave him an odd look.

Bollocks! He was acting like a green boy! "Uh, yes. Yes, we've been introduced and move in the same circles. Did you receive an invitation from them? Their affairs are usually such a crush."

"Oh, my. I have no desire to be packed into a room like sheep in a shearing pen. Goodness, I would be ready to head back to Pendleton Place, then."

"I have some excellent news. Mama has secured three vouchers to Almack's for this Wednesday next," announced Mattie. "We may each bring a guest so we shall all go together."

Mattie's cheeks were pink from the unaccustomed wine, and the fact she'd just put all attention on her. She hated being in the center of anything, but here she was prattling on. It warmed his heart and he had an idea who was responsible for this sudden buoyancy.

His gaze again wandered to Miss Pendleton, his sister's words a pleasant hum. She was a good companion for Mattie. He'd engaged her in several conversations and enjoyed her company. He was surprised Stanfeld had not noticed how she'd blossomed into such a beauty. Well read but not opinionated, kind but witty with a good humor, and optimistic but practical.

If he'd been in the market for a wife, he'd have considered her. But he wasn't and needed to get his desire under control. Miss Hannah Pendleton was young and innocent, and despite his attraction to her, he needed to remain detached.

"Oh, no. My mother said we shall come round and pick you up in the town coach. I must say, I was dreading an evening at Almack's, but now I can barely contain myself." Mattie's blue eyes shone with excitement. He couldn't remember the last time she had seemed so animated outside their home. "With my two good friends beside me, it should be a splendid evening."

"Who else is accompanying us?" asked Lady Roberta. "You said she'd received three vouchers. A friend of Lady Darby?"

"Oh, my brother. Mama said it would be good for him to reintroduce himself to quality ladies instead..." Her eyes went wide with horror as she looked at her brother. "I didn't mean, er, I meant—"

"It's quite all right, Mattie." He turned to Lady Roberta, unable to meet Hannah's eyes. "I have been a lonely widower for the past five years and have not stepped foot near Almack's. It is where I met my wife, you see." He hoped this didn't quiet Matilda. She'd been so vivacious.

Miss Pendleton's hand touched his arm and like an unseen force, his eyes were pulled to her face. Those pools of amber and brown held such emotion. But not pity, thank God. He hated pity. He saw a gentle, enveloping compassion in her expression that made him want to bury his face in her neck and feel her hands stroke his head. *Egads!* The liquor was making a buffoon out of him.

"Then isn't it opportune that we can all go together?" she asked softly, sending a quick smile to Mattie. "You won't have to cross that bridge alone. Things are so much easier with friends, are they not?" And she squeezed his arm.

"Yes, I suppose so," he mumbled, staring at the long slender fingers on his sleeve.

"What is our first game of the evening, Aunt Bertie?" asked Pendleton, patting his stomach. "Please don't make it anything too difficult. Between the excellent meal and the brandy I'm about to share with Darby, I won't be a quick study."

"We'll retire and get the games ready," said Miss Pendleton, rising. "We will see you gentlemen soon."

The ladies retreated and Pendleton rose to pour the brandy. "You seem attentive to my sister."

"She's a lovely woman." Nicholas wanted to turn this subject quickly. "I'm sure she'll find a suitable match before the season is out."

"Yes, I hope so. I realize she's your sort, er, physically. I've seen several of your mistresses." He handed Darby a glass. "But you have promised to protect her.

With a chuckle, he sipped the brandy. "Even if it's from myself. Yes, I understand, my friend. I'll not let her charms overwhelm me."

"Behold the wooden plate," announced Lady Roberta to the small group assembled in the drawing room. "Typically, we would Twirl the Trencher on the floor, and the spinner would call out a name and that person would catch the plate before it stopped spinning."

"Yes, Aunt Bertie," said Pendleton. "We all know how to play."

"I have added a *twist* to the game," she said with an impish grin, holding the plate up and spinning it on the tip of her forefinger. "You must spin the plate like so." She demonstrated again, her agility impressive as she balanced the platter in motion. "And keep it spinning while you call out someone's name. They must collect the plate and keep it spinning as you transfer it from one hand to the next. If the plate falls, they both forfeit."

"What a clever turnabout," exclaimed Hannah. "Who begins and what do we forfeit?"

"A secret or a shilling because I have plenty of both." Lady Roberta clapped her hands. "The plate must never touch the floor but you can touch it to keep it from falling or to keep it spinning. But once you call the name, it must spin on its own."

"I'll begin." Pendleton stood in the center of the group and held the plate up. It took him several attempts, holding his finger at different angles before he called, "Hannah!"

She dashed forward and placed her finger under the plate just as it began to wobble. With a flick of her wrist, she sent it twirling again as her brother stepped back. Her giggles were contagious as she tried to keep the plate moving, and soon they were all laughing. When the wooden disc hit the floor, Miss Pendleton gave a little squeal.

"Oh, my. A shilling or secret?" Her finger pushed against her bottom lip as her foot tapped the carpet. "I shall share a secret. I am afraid of the dark."

"Really?" asked Mattie. "What do you do at night? Have your lady's maid sleep with you? You can't keep a candle burning all night long."

Miss Pendleton laughed. "Oh, goodness no. I hate the pitch black. I leave the shades open at night so the moonlight gives me some relief. If it's an especially dark night, I don't bank the coals, and the glow from the embers are enough."

Her brother explained, "We found a cave once while exploring our property. I was home from university and Stanfeld had come to visit. Hannah was only, what? Eight years old?"

She nodded her agreement. "I was teasing Nathaniel, trying to act like an adult and impress Gideon. I snatched the torch and ran into the cave. It had several tunnels. I tripped, the torch fell, and I was in utter darkness. It was horrible."

"I could hear her screaming and desperately searched for another stick, anything to make another torch to find her."

"What happened?" Mattie asked, her eyes wide. "Did Lord Pendleton save you?"

"Well, she continued to scream, 'Something touched me. There's scratching on the walls!' I tell you, it put a shiver down my spine."

"There was something touching me. Gideon finally made some fire and found me. He pulled the spider from my hair." Her hands flew to her chignon as if checking to make sure it was truly gone. "Then we saw the walls were covered in bats. Completely covered. I thought I would faint, so Gideon swept me into his arms and carried me to safety." She sighed as if reliving a wonderful dream.

Nicholas's stomach inexplicably tightened at the thought of Gideon acting as the knight saving the damsel in distress. *Bollocks! Don't be a greenboy.*

They played several more games, then Miss Pendleton played the pianoforte for them. Her fingers danced and teased the keys. Her eyes closed as her fingers coaxed a haunting melody from the ivories, a smile curving her rosy mouth. Nicholas longed to be those keys and feel the soft touch of her skin against his. She was exquisite.

Afterward, Lady Roberta played and tempted the younger members with a country dance.

"Lady Matilda, may I have this dance?" asked Nathaniel with a bow.

Mattie curtsied and extended her hand. "It would be my pleasure, sir."

"Miss Pendleton? May I have the honor?" he asked, taking Pendleton's lead.

"Certainly," she agreed and took her place.

She was graceful and light on her feet, and Nicholas realized how much he'd missed dancing. He was sorry to see the evening end, and he hadn't been able to say that in a very long time.

On the way home, Mattie laid her head against his shoulder. "Did you have a good time tonight?"

"Yes, I'm surprised to say, I did. Lady Roberta is certainly an engaging hostess." He kissed the top of her head. "And you?"

"I shall be very lonely when Hannah leaves. She's fine as a fivepence, is she not?"

He chuckled. "Yes, I believe she is."

"Do you like her then?" Mattie's tone was nonchalant but he knew better.

"I do, as the sister of my very good friend, *and* the very good friend of my favorite sister." He thought it best to change the subject. "Have you decided what to wear to the masquerade next week? Is Mother taking you shopping?"

Nicholas watched his sister, prattling on about her costume as any young girl might, entering the marriage mart. The transformation in her the past couple weeks was astonishing. How many times had he tried to bring her out of her shell? How many times had his mother introduced her to other girls, only to find her sitting quietly, head down, avoiding attention of any kind?

"I hope to meet Lord Pendleton's wife and daughter one day," Mattie was saying. "Perhaps this summer we could take a trip to the country? Hannah has extended a formal invitation."

"I'm sure we can arrange it," Nicholas murmured. "Let's just get through this year first." His mind had turned to the meeting with Walters later at the Guinea.

Another social call into St. Giles if his hunch was correct. After that, a bottle of whatever was at hand, anguished promises of revenge to a dead woman, and then blissful numbness. A month of escape, self-blame, cursing conniving women, and drowning in the inequity of Fate. One month out of twelve when he took the time to feel sorry for himself. It had become a ritual that he despised but couldn't seem to break.

"Perhaps this year will be better," Mattie said, squeezing his hand and misinterpreting his silence, "with our new friends and the hectic social whirl Mama is planning."

He leaned his head back against the squab. Yes, the dreaded December was upon them. *No, sweet sister*, he thought, *it would not be better*. This time of the year would always be a nightmare for him. It would begin the first of December, the day he had proposed to Alice. It would continue each night until the next year. By Twelfth Night, five years ago, the inquiry had been completed; his wife had been declared fragile of mind and could not be held responsible for her actions.

The husband was thus allowed to retain her dowry and properties. His financial ruin had been resolved, and it was as if his marriage had never happened because no one uttered a word about it again. To his face. Except Mattie. The only person who dared speak of it. The only person who knew of the anguish that annually drowned his soul. The only person who knew he had a heart that was permanently cracked and deformed and loved him anyway. Yes, he would do anything for his sister.

CHAPTER SIX

ONCE UPON A WIDOW©

"If once to Almack's you belong,

    Like monarchs, you can do no wrong;

    But banished thence on Wednesday night,

    By Jove you can do nothing right."

— HENRY LUTTRELL, *ADVICE TO JULIA*

Almack's
First week of December 1819

$\mathcal{T}$he large building on King's Street was nothing spectacular. A rather stuffy-looking building, in Hannah's opinion, with the obligatory wrought-iron fence at the street and arched windows on the second story. But inside, Almack's was just as her mother had described.

Mattie squeezed her hand as they entered a large rectangular room decorated with gilded columns, and lines of red velvet ropes to designate an area for dancing. Chairs bordered the room, and behind them mirrors covered the walls. A balcony held the musicians, warming up for the first dance set. A dais was set up with chairs for the patronesses to oversee and approve of the guests and happenings. One word from an Almack's patroness could ruin a debutante's hopes of a good match. These women also decided the dance partners for the young hopeful females. This was the place to mingle with the most eligible bachelors in Town.

The room was already filled with men in dark coats, black knee breeches, silk stockings, and the obligatory white cravat. The women added the color to the room. Their gowns sported every fashionable color, solid and print, embellished with bows, embroidery, and beads emphasizing high waists, hems, and cuffs. Under the gas-lit chandeliers, gems glittered at their throats and fingers, in tiaras and hair combs artfully placed within the elaborate curls. Some women wore turbans, and all wore gloves.

"I see why the magazines call this the seventh heaven of the fashionable world," said Hannah, trying not to gape at the *beau monde* turned out for Almack's first ball of the season.

Lady Darby led the way in a silk gown of bottle green with an overdress of Apollo gold. Hannah felt like a newborn foal trailing after its mother as they moved in and out of the crowd, following the trembling feather on Lady Darby's gold turban. Hannah and Mattie walked with linked arms, Aunt Bertie following. When they reached the dais, Lady Cowper, one of Almack's patronesses, met them.

"Ah, Lady Darby, so this is your lovely daughter." Lady Cowper's shrewd blue eyes took in the ladies. She was a striking woman with dark hair, pink cheeks, and a rosebud mouth. "I'm happy to welcome you, Lady Matilda."

"It's an honor, ma'am," Mattie said with a slight curtsy. "May I introduce—"

"Lady Roberta, is that you?" Lady Cowper beamed and hurried down the several steps, her arms outstretched. "Where *have* you been hiding?"

Lady Darby looked as though she might have an apoplexy, realizing the patroness was on such good terms with Lady Roberta.

"You will have to tell me of your latest adventures so I can relay all the information back to William," the patroness gushed, taking Bertie's arm and giving it a squeeze. "And may I say this Devonshire brown really sets off your hair. I'm so glad you are not hiding those dark waves in a turban."

Lady Darby blanched, touching her own turban, and Hannah bit back a smile at the countess' pinched mouth.

"Oh, my dear," said Aunt Bertie to Lady Cowper, "what a beauty you've become. And how is your dear brother? I was so sorry to hear of his troubles." She flapped a hand at her niece. "Come here, my dear. I'd like you to meet the sister of an old friend of mine. This is Emily, Lady Cowper. This is my niece, Lady Hannah Pendleton, here for her first season in London."

"It is a pleasure indeed. We shall see each other often, I hope." She turned back to Aunt Bertie. "Are you chaperoning, then?"

"Yes, and looking forward to it."

"I will send an invitation for dinner. Now I must be off to oversee the other guests." Lady Cowper gave them all a smile and moved on. "I'll send your cards over before the dancing begins."

They made their way across the room for a cup of Almack's infamous horrid lemonade, following Mattie and her mother.

"Aunt Bertie, I thought Lady Darby would faint just now. Always a trick up your sleeve, eh? She had no idea you were on speaking terms with Almack's royalty." Hannah searched the room for a familiar face. "I thought Gideon might be here."

As she spoke the words, another face appeared in the sea

of bodies. A golden head with a cleft in his chin and smiling blue eyes.

"What luck! The four most beautiful ladies in the room all in one spot. My search is over." Lord Darby bowed before them.

Hannah was surprised to find herself blushing again. He was not what she typically considered handsome, preferring Gideon's dark handsome looks to such blond, fair features. Yet, the attraction was undeniable. Considering his reputation, she decided he would be a safe flirtation. Heaven knew she needed the practice, her only experience being with the young village boys or a couple of squires' sons. "Will you be dancing tonight, Lord Darby?"

"I believe that is a prerequisite to any bachelor who crosses the threshold. Perhaps I shall be fortunate enough to stand across from you." Another gentleman waved to him from the side of the room. "If my ladies will excuse me, I must speak with someone."

Again, Hannah met so many people during the next few hours; she was thankful for Aunt Bertie, who never forgot a name or a face. She and Mattie had been assigned the second set, and Hannah found herself dancing a quadrille with a young baronet, tall and lanky with a long face that reminded her of a horse. When he smiled, his teeth were almost as large.

After a second dance, Mattie begged her partner for a cup of lemonade and Hannah asked for the same. Her present dancing companion was pleasant enough, with a round face and kind brown eyes. He had not stepped on her foot or missed a step throughout the dance, unlike her first partner.

As they waited, she saw Gideon. Waving over the crowd, almost hopping on her tiptoes, she caught his attention. His smile sent her stomach tumbling. "Lord Stanfeld! I am so happy to see you. I've been wondering when you would make London."

"I've only arrived this week, dear lady, and planned on calling soon." He bowed to Mattie. "Lady Matilda, it is a pleasure to see you again."

They traded news of their respective families, and then Hannah inquired about her competition. "I heard you brought someone back from Scotland."

And with that, the quiet and thoughtful earl launched into a ten-minute description of the glorious, intelligent, sweetly demure, and most beautiful Scottish lass he had met in the Highlands. The wings in her stomach turned to stone as she watched his eyes and heard the affection in his voice. He was in love with her. It was obvious to anyone who knew him. Gideon would not gush over an infatuation. No, this was genuine love.

As he walked away, Hannah blinked rapidly, pushing back the disappointment. She had thought she would be angry with him, jealous of this widow who'd stolen his heart. Instead, her heart was heavy, but she was happy for him. Gideon had never looked so vibrant. Did he have any idea how his news had affected her? She took a deep breath and raised her chin, determined to never let him see her disappointment.

As they sipped lemonade, another attractive dark-haired man approached them. His black eyes glittered, his raven hair slicked back and perfectly in place. His features were chiseled and as his eyes traveled over her, a chill went through her despite the warmth in the crowded room. He stood next to them without speaking, but she knew he studied them. The scent of lavender and peppermint assailed her, and she wrinkled her nose. What an odd combination.

A warm breath tickled her ear when the stranger whispered, "You seem familiar. Have we met before?"

She gave him a side glance and shook her head. "I'm afraid not. So we'll have to wait until formally introduced."

At that moment, the horse man, her first dance partner, arrived. The dark stranger seemed to know him and introductions were soon made. At the mention of the Duke of Colvin, Mattie clutched Hannah's arm. She turned to her friend and was appalled to see her so pale, her eyes wide as she stared at the nobleman.

"My apologies, Lady Matilda," he said with a formal bow. "I did not realize who you were or I would never have put you in such an awkward position." He turned to Hannah. "It seems the son will always be punished for the sins of the father."

"I'm sorry to hear that Your Grace," Hannah murmured as she tucked Mattie's arm in hers. "If you'll excuse us—"

"He should be excusing himself," Darby interrupted. "What the hell do you think you're doing?" he hissed at the duke.

"As I told the lovely Miss Pendleton, I did not realize they were in your company. However, I do not think you have the authority to restrict where I go or who I converse with. Beware of your tone and remember who I am, *Lord* Darby." His black eyes glittered and a humorless smile curved his lips.

Though Colvin's manners had been acceptable, she had the impression he'd known exactly what he was doing. He'd gotten under Darby's skin with a look and a few words. The earl's jaw clenched, his amiable expression gone and replaced with something akin to hatred. An emotion she'd never felt toward another person. While the circumstances indicated a son wronged because of his father's actions, this scene spoke of other past sins. She put her arm around Mattie and was thankful when Lady Darby and Aunt Bertie appeared.

"My dear girls, shall we get our feet and see what stale

repast might be offered?" asked Aunt Bertie. "It's all part of the experience, don't you know!"

Nicholas struggled to calm his temper, but the scoundrel had gone too far. What in God's name was he doing here? Colvin had no interest in debutantes or Almack's. And to approach his sister... Oh how he wanted to draw his cork. A vision of blood spurting from the man's nose gave him some calm. What did he know? Or suspect?

Walters had kept someone on him, detailing his movements, hoping to find something, anything to bring against him. So far, the duke's weekly trips into St. Giles had produced nothing. Colvin would emerge from a nondescript coach, enter the slash house, and go to a private room. He would quietly drink his ale and be shown several different boys. So far, the duke had not gone any further. Darby was patient.

Then tonight he showed up here. The thought of that sordid ogre in the same room as Mattie terrified him. With an effort, he sucked air into his lungs and forced a smile on his face. He would need a long session at Jackson's to expel this tension. In the meantime, he'd find Stanfeld. The man always had a flask in his pocket for such occasions.

A few swallows of whiskey and several thin sandwiches later, Nicholas had relaxed and was enjoying a description of Miss Pendleton's two dance partners. She had a way of describing a person or situation with humor without being hurtful, usually beginning or finishing a story by making fun of herself. He found himself chuckling despite the previous incident and realized he liked this girl.

It startled him, for it had been a long time since he'd even considered another female in such a way. As a possible friend. She was enticing tonight in a champagne gown that matched her eyes, and garnets gleaming a deep red brown in her hair and at her throat.

Later in the evening, a waltz was announced. Miss Pendleton seemed to search for someone, before her eyes darkened and she looked down as if remembering something sad. He bowed. "Miss Pendleton, I believe you promised me the first waltz."

She looked at him, blinking several times, and gave him a watery smile. "Yes, you are correct, my lord." She laid her fingers on his sleeve, and he guided her to the dance floor.

As his arm went around her waist, their eyes locked. "My lady, I am usually adept at making women laugh. Yet, I glimpse a melancholy in your eyes. Are my charms fading?"

She laughed softly, a husky sound that made his heart pound. "No, my lord, your appeal is strong. I was just thinking of someone."

"Stanfeld, perhaps?"

"Horsefeathers! My brother told you!" Her features hardened in mock anger, but the unhappiness had lifted. "I realized that my first love has found another. I'm not sure if I'm more disappointed about Gideon or the fact that I'm truly one of those girls searching for a husband."

He put his head back and laughed. "What an awful thought. And here I thought myself extremely clever at avoiding those girls. You've trapped me, Miss Pendleton." He grinned, enjoying the feel of her hand in his, her waist as they moved and swirled together.

"Don't look down, my lord," she said with a smirk. "You'll see the leg shackles I secretly attached."

He cocked his head. "Ah, that was the faint rattle of chains I heard."

Her laughter filled him with...contentment. There was an easiness in her company that made him want to spend time with her, banter with her, watch her. The way her eyes lit up when she thought of something clever, or the way she chewed her bottom lip when she was deep in thought. As Nicholas turned them from the path of another couple, he spotted Colvin leaning against the wall. His eyes followed them, a faint smile on his lips. *What was he up to?*

The music ended and Hannah stilled, her hand on her chest as she caught her breath. Her flushed face, her mouth slightly opened, her heaving chest, all had a devastating impact on Darby. His eyes moved from her full lips to the creamy mounds below her neckline, and back to her face. Shock flared in her eyes and he realized his hand was still on her waist. If they'd been alone, he would have pulled her to him and tasted the sweet temptation before him. His friend's words echoed in his head.

I need you to protect her, not ogle her.

He dropped his hand and bowed deeply. "Miss Pendleton, I hope I did justice to your first waltz."

"Oh, yes," she said breathlessly, sending fire to his loins, "more than you know."

Nicholas had sent the ladies on their way and was waiting for his own coach. His mistress would be at the Wicked Earls' Club, and he needed a release. And brandy. Lots of it.

"Your sister is quite a pretty little thing, Darby. A bit too mousy for my taste, though."

The voice of the duke behind him sent a wave of disgust through Nicholas. "Stay away," he grumbled through gritted teeth.

"Stay away. Seems like excellent advice a man should keep for himself." He stepped up next to Nicholas. "I'm wondering why an earl would have me followed. Hmm. I highly doubt it has to do with a card game my father played." He put his hat on and pulled on one glove. "No, I think it might be a bit more personal than that."

Nicholas stood rigid, cursing the driver for taking so long with the coach.

"So I ask myself, could he possible know about"—the duke leaned close to Nicholas's face—"*sweet Alice.*"

Darby swung around but Colvin had already stepped back, his white teeth showing in a cruel resemblance of a smile. "Ah, I think he might. Well," the duke continued as he put on the other glove, "I should warn you that I may be getting a craving for that kind of thing again."

"If you ever touch a hair on my sister's head—"

"Oh, no. As I said, she's not quite my type. I prefer a little more fight. It's Miss Pendleton I have my eye on." Colvin's carriage pulled up. "Let's make a truce. I'll stay in my neighborhood of choice, if you stay in yours."

"Keep away from what's mine." Nicholas had grown cold. The thought of an innocent in the duke's hands sickened him. He wanted to wrap his fingers around the nobleman's throat and squeeze the life from him.

"Oh, so now she is yours? Hmm. I've found myself to be quite adept at reading people. I saw what passed between the two of you during the dance. I hadn't realized your affections had progressed so far."

"She is under my protection." He took a step closer, nose to nose to with Colvin. "In your own words, I do not think you have the authority to restrict where I go or who I converse with. Beware of your tone and remember who *I* am, *Your Grace.*"

"It seems we are at odds then," the duke relented. "Just remember, to the victor goes the spoils."

CHAPTER SEVEN

"Time heals griefs and quarrels, for we change and are no longer the same persons. Neither the offender nor the offended are any more themselves."

— BLAISE PASCAL

Wicked Earls' Club
Mid-December 1819

icholas sank into the leather chair, the cheerful fire irritating his foul mood. His mistress had left the upstairs room in a storm when he'd cut it off with her. He hadn't wanted to end it so suddenly, though he'd been thinking about it for the last few weeks. But his conversation with Colvin had hurried the matter along. If the duke was having Nicholas followed, she could also be an unintended victim. It was better to send her off now.

"Darby, you're foxed again." Stanfeld sat down next to him and picked up a decanter of amber liquid sitting between them on the floor. "I realize it's a festive month, Christmas and Yuletide and all that, but have a care. You almost knocked this perfectly good bottle of brandy on the carpet."

Nicholas grunted. "I've had enough, so help yourself. I need to find my way *home* tonight."

"You're back to staying at the townhouse?"

"My mother doesn't want any kind of scandal during Mattie's first season. So, I'm staying in my father's rooms for now. I shan't quit the club." Nicholas had never stepped foot in his old rooms since his wedding night. He doubted he ever would.

Stanfeld poured himself a glass. "Giving up this club is *almost* a reason not to get married. However, I think I'll be lured into the parson's trap by this time next year. Perhaps a best friend's wedding in December will give you better memories."

Nicholas grunted again. "You broke Hannah's heart tonight."

"It's Hannah already, is it?" Stanfeld asked softly.

"Only in my mind."

"I broke a little girl's heart tonight, not the woman you danced with."

"What's that supposed to mean?" Nicholas wasn't in the mood for riddles.

"I was what the five-year-old Hannah always wanted. Like the fox kit she thought she wanted to tame when she was ten. Once it bit her, she realized what she really wanted was a dog, a companion or pet." Stanfeld grinned. "While the child may have dreamed about Gideon, the woman will be dreaming about Darby tonight."

"What makes you think that?"

"As I've said, I've known her since she was five. You seduced her with a waltz." He shook his head. "I don't know how, but one dance and I saw it in her face. I was nothing but a memory after all these years."

Nicholas laughed. "You are as fickle as a woman. Make up your mind, you bufflehead."

"I'll say the same to you. As a friend." Stanfeld's voice lowered. "She's Pendleton's sister, remember. Don't play with her affections unless you are serious."

"I know, I know." Nicholas leaned forward, his elbows on his knees, his face in his hands. "She is special, though. And Mattie adores her."

"Then get over your dead wife and stop blaming yourself for what you couldn't control. It was a tragedy and you, my friend, were as much a victim as she was."

He felt a hand grip his shoulder.

"Forgive yourself," Stanfeld said, "and then forgive her. Or you'll never be able to love another."

Later in his father's rooms, Nicholas sat slumped in front of another hearth, the rest of the brandy gone, a paper in his hand. His vision blurred as he looked at the writing, but he knew what the words said. He'd memorized Alice's last note long ago. Retribution was close, so close. But now others were involved. Could he risk the safety of someone like Hannah in order to bring down the duke?

The man was as slimy and slippery as the back alleys of the rookeries. He needed to find evidence of a crime and stop this noxious worm. When Colvin had moved on from decent society and satiated himself in gin houses, Nicholas had breathed a sigh of relief for the innocents of the *ton*. The harlots of Covent Garden made their own decisions and were well paid for their discomfort. Not that he agreed with any of it, but it was the way of the world.

Now the fiend was going after children. His heart of stone was cracking as he thought of the children so often abducted in the streets and alleys of the city. Or worse, sold by the crooked orphanages or parents to feed the rest of the family. He couldn't save the world; he couldn't even save most of those children, but he would keep them from the hands of that evil monster Colvin. He would give them a fighting chance to survive.

Pendleton townhouse

Hannah settled into the overstuffed chair and picked up her book of poems. Shelley was one of her favorites, and it was a perfect afternoon for reading. Aunt Bertie worked on a dissected map puzzle of Africa.

After an hour of companionable silence, Aunt Bertie called her over to the table. "Come help me with this puzzle, my dear, and we can talk. We need to discuss some things you might overhear in the future."

"Yes, Mama said to ignore any gossip about our family."

The older woman rolled her eyes. "Your family skeletons have long been swept under the carpet. There have been hundreds of scandals to replace the *Pendleton's Public Disgrace* as it was once called." She gave Hannah's fingers a squeeze as she sat down in front of the lower half of Africa. "One day, your mama and I will sit down and have a long talk. It's past time she put aside her resentment of my brother *and* myself."

"What do you mean?" asked Hannah. A nervous excitement filled her. Would she finally learn the details of her father's death? Of the whispers that had made her mother avoid London as if the plague still lurked in its streets and alleys?

She only knew the barest of facts. Father had been unfaithful to Mama, caught with a married woman, and challenged to a duel. Since he'd never been a good shot, it had not ended well. He'd died a few days later from a chest wound.

"Nathaniel informed me before he left that your mother has taken her share of responsibility for the tragedy. You should know what has been said, and what is the truth, before you hear any exaggerations."

"The truth?" A disquiet settled over the room as Hannah studied her aunt's face.

"Yes, and the beginning is the best place to start." She pushed back from the table, resettled the cap on her head, and placed her hands in her lap. "Did you know your mother was first pursued by your uncle? My oldest brother?"

Hannah shook her head.

"It never reached a formal betrothal before his accident, so many did not know. My oldest brother was not as handsome as your father. He was a rigid man and good with figures. The estate prospered under his care." She paused.

"He would have made a good husband for your mother. She had certain expectations, and he would have fulfilled them. It may not have been a love match, but the marriage would have been successful in many other ways. They were...compatible."

"And my mother and father were not?"

Aunt Bertie pursed her lips then let out a heavy sigh. "No, I'm afraid not. Your father was never raised to take on the title, and he had no head for accounts or the running of an estate. He was a generous soul, to be sure, and tended to give away money to help the tenants rather than make the estate prosperous to benefit everyone.

"Your mother was captivated by his looks and easy charm at first. She thought herself the luckiest of women, winning the most handsome man of the season along with a prosperous estate and other holdings. But it didn't last long."

"Nathaniel remembered them getting along before I was

born," added Hannah. "She was beautiful back then, he said, smiling often and even laughing."

Aunt Bertie nodded. "Yes, but then one bad investment after another emptied the coffers. Lady Pendleton would rant and rave at him, sending him from the house. He stayed away for longer and longer intervals to escape her constant criticism. As he was seen more in town, the gossip began. Your mother was cast as a sharp tongue, driving her husband away, pushing him into the arms of others. It wasn't true of course. Your father was a social creature and a natural flirt. But tongues wagged."

"My poor mother," exclaimed Hannah. "No wonder she avoids the Town."

"One of the loudest voices was Lady Darby. She had always carried a torch for your father and had never let go of her jealousy toward your mother."

"Mattie's mother?" Hannah gasped. "She and my mother are enemies?"

"I wouldn't go to that extreme, but they are certainly not friends."

"The last time my brother went home to Pendleton Place, there was a terrible argument. Your mother said things she didn't mean, and he was finally worn down. Escaping to London, he found comfort in the arms of a countess. A wicked woman who had been trying to seduce your father for a year. They were caught, and—"

"He was challenged to a duel," finished Hannah. "Oh, my. That's quite a tale."

"Yes, and in your mother's defense, she wished with all her heart she could have taken back her words. Your father was a disappointment to her but she did care for him. I believe that with all my heart. He just could never be the man she needed, so both were miserable together."

"How tragic. It explains so much, though." She looked at

Aunt Bertie. "But Nathaniel has done what Father could not. I'm sure he's smiling down on us now."

Aunt Bertie shrugged. "He had help. Without your estate manager, Maxwell, he may well have floundered too. Your brother was only twelve when he inherited the title."

Hannah shook her head. "He was born to be Viscount. He inherited the best of both our parents."

"Both of you have. My brother would be so proud of his children."

Hannah wiped at her eyes and accepted the hug from her aunt. "Thank you for telling me. If I hear any whispers, I will keep my head high and ignore them. But what of Lady Darby? Why would she agree to assist with my coming out?"

"Guilt, perhaps, hoping to make amends. I've accepted that olive branch, so don't give it another thought." She smiled and tilted her head, her eyes narrowing. "Now, tell me of Lord Darby and your waltz last night."

Hannah studied her cuff, picking at a thread. "There's nothing to tell. We danced, it was lovely, and then it was over."

"It seemed a bit more than that. I swear he wasn't going to let you go!" She beamed at her niece. "Not that I blame him. Who could resist you?"

Hannah blushed. "You are prejudiced, Aunt, and I thank you for it. But I fear the earl reminds me too much of my own father. We are not suited." Hannah paused, resuming her attention to the loose thread on her cuff. "I heard some girls talking after the waltz. They spoke of his mistresses. His present one is married, you know."

Aunt Bertie nodded. "I see. Many men have mistresses before they are betrothed. It…simplifies things for them. Many men also keep them afterward. It all depends on the man."

"I don't care since I'm not interested. Nathaniel has

warned me away from him. I think it's good advice, though I will continue to enjoy his company."

"As you will," Aunt Bertie said, "but remember, people are not always as they seem. I suspect there is much more to Lord Darby than he allows us to see."

The rest of the afternoon was spent making plans for the upcoming holiday. There were mince pies being prepared in the kitchen, a masquerade over the weekend, and countless invitations to go through. Aunt Bertie helped her decide which requests to accept and which to decline.

As she snuggled under the heavy counterpane that night, watching the snow fall against the window, she replayed the waltz over in her mind. It had been dizzying bliss. It had been shocking. It had been exactly what she'd hoped for when she had dreamed of her first waltz. But it had not been Gideon who sent her heart racing and made her mouth go dry. Lord Darby was quite the opposite in coloring and disposition. Hannah hadn't wanted the music to end, and it seemed Lord Darby had not wanted it to end either.

She thought of her time so far in London and what she had discovered about herself and others. Mattie had seemed a timid girl when they'd first met, but her friend had a quiet competence that kept Hannah grounded. Aunt Bertie had revealed that Hannah's mother had not been the victim she'd been led to believe all her life.

Her attraction to Gideon had faded quickly in the bright lights of London, and his reserved character had been changed by his love for another. Perhaps Darby was not quite the uncaring rake after all. Perhaps he presented the face he needed to, in order to cope with the horrific hand that he'd been dealt. No, she decided, there would be no quick judgments anymore. People were much more complicated than Hannah had ever realized.

CHAPTER EIGHT

"Variety's the very spice of life, that gives it all its flavour."

— *"THE TIMEPIECE" THE TASK, II, 1785, LINES*
606–7

Pendleton townhouse
Mid-December 1819

"Oh, yes! Let's play Feather Shuttlecock!" cried Mattie.
"Who has a feather?"

They were gathered at the Pendleton townhouse. The
faces of the other guests were familiar, and Hannah was
beginning to recognize people during their shopping outings
or rides in Hyde Park. Tonight, a baron, his wife, and two
daughters were among the added members of their group.

Lady Roberta pulled one from her turban. "And I have
more where that came from," she said, bobbing her head with
a giggle.

The group stood in the center of the drawing room and
formed a circle. The baron's wife began by placing the

peacock feather on her palm and blowing it toward her husband. He blew at it, turning red in the face, but it went toward the center. His daughter ran forward, crouched below as it fell, and blew it toward Hannah. She stepped forward and blew it at Nicholas.

As Nicholas watched her lips pucker and form an O, his pulse raced. He watched as the feather went straight up into the air and back toward that delectable mouth. Desire pounded him like a hard beating in the ring. Then the blasted feather hit him in the face and fell to the ground.

"First one out must pour me a drink," called out the baron. "I'm happy not to be the first one out for a change."

Nicholas obliged and then settled back in the chair, watching the game progress. He decided he preferred being a spectator. From this view, Hannah's backside was presented to him, and every time she bent or twisted...

"I see you, Lord Darby," said Lady Roberta with a titter. "Not that I blame you."

She sat down next to him and watched the remaining players with him. It was down to the girls and they were laughing and blowing the poor feather every which way.

"I beg your pardon," Nicholas admitted with a grin. "Or her pardon."

"If I didn't know better, I'd think you were becoming quite fond of our Hannah." She gave him a sidelong glance. "But of course, we all know Darby has no interest in a wife. He only cares for meaningless flirtations."

Nicholas cleared his throat. "So true, ma'am. So true." He would let this dog lie.

"And we both know that's a clanker. You may sham yourself, but I didn't cut my eye teeth yesterday." She leaned closer. "If it makes a difference, I think she's quite taken with you. Of course, she's also pretending she's not. Two peas in a pod, both of you."

With that, Lady Roberta walked away and left Nicholas with his mouth open. Feather Shuttlecock ended, and Mattie called out for music. Hannah took a seat at the pianoforte, her skill on the keys no longer a secret.

"Shall we begin practicing for Christmas?" she asked. Everyone murmured agreement and she began with "Hark! The Herald Angels Sing."

Nicholas watched her fingers lightly stroke the ivories, her head swaying to the rhythm of the song. Dark honey curls fell from a chignon and gently caressed her slender neck. As she played, voices joined in, and without thought, he began to hum. It had been years since he'd sung a holiday melody. It lightened his heart a bit, and his eyes caught Hannah's. She smiled at him as she continued to play and sing with the group. His stomach knotted.

She could break your heart.

The piece of stone in his chest would shatter and never be mended. Or could she patch it up? Save what's left of it? Miss Pendleton was haunting his dreams now. He would wake in a sweat, hard and aching, with her face before his eyes. He tried to blame it on the fact he'd dismissed his mistress.

The song ended, and Mattie called out a request. "If you please, 'God Rest Ye Merry, Gentlemen' with Nicholas singing the verses and the rest of us taking the chorus."

He jerked at the mention of his name and the urging of the group. "I'll agree only if my sister accompanies me on the harp." Nicholas enjoyed her blush, and they both went to the corner of the room where the harp stood. Hannah left the piano to join the others. Would he remember the lyrics? It had been so long.

With the first strum of the harp strings, the words came back to him. He had a deep baritone that lent to this particular song well. As he took the air in and sang another verse, he felt her eyes on him.

She had a faint smile on her face as she watched him, and surprise in her eyes, he thought, at his voice. Her gaze sent heat rushing from his chest to his groin, and he found himself enjoying the moment. The holiday song, a beautiful woman's lingering gaze, wondering if it were possible to fall in love again. To trust another woman. If it were, it would be Miss Hannah Pendleton.

Hannah listened to the resonant tones as Darby sang the carol. It was perfect for his deep timbre. He looked so handsome, so golden and perfect as he stood next to Mattie and sang the lyrics. His voice sent a warmth through her that made her knees weak and her heart race.

She had studied him over the last week since Almack's. There was so much more beneath that polished exterior. She'd seen pain in his eyes, quickly covered with indifference. Her heart longed to soothe him, her affections growing after each encounter, despite her inner objections. Despite the warnings of her brother and the insensitive gossips.

"Bravo!" Aunt Bertie clapped enthusiastically. "Another, we beg you for one more."

Darby shook his head, and Mattie deferred to Hannah. "Miss Pendleton is much more capable than I."

"I will play as long as I have the sheet music." Hannah moved back to the bench and was pleased when Darby followed her.

"I'll be happy to turn the page for you, my lady." He gave her a bow and a wink, which sent her stomach into a flutter.

Hannah began the opening notes of "Deck the Halls" and sucked in a breath as the earl leaned over her, ready to flip the page. His breath feathered her hair and sent a shiver down her arms. What would his lips feel like against her skin? His cheek against hers? *Stop it!* Oh, she was a wanton woman with such thoughts. Her cheeks burned with the indecent thoughts and she was thankful when the song ended.

"Are you well?" he whispered close to her ear. A masculine scent, leather and musk with a hint of vanilla, lingered on his skin. "You look flushed."

Hannah looked up and those eyes, such a soft clear blue, seemed to see right through her. Right through to her heart. He lifted a hand; his knuckles moved toward her cheek and then froze. Their gazes locked. A dull throb began low in her belly, spreading and thudding inside her. *Horsefeathers!* How she wanted him to kiss her. Had he really almost touched her?

"A game of whist, anyone?" called out Aunt Bertie.

The moment was broken. When Hannah looked at her aunt, she smiled and raised an eyebrow. *Piffle! She saw it.*

The baron and his wife declined as did Darby. Hannah decided she couldn't concentrate on the game and joined the others by the fireplace. The younger girls and Aunt Bertie sat a table and began the game.

"Miss Pendleton, would you care to take a turn around the room?" The earl was smiling, the dimple deepening as the smile grew. "I believe a bit of exercise would do us both good."

"A splendid idea," she agreed and took his hand to rise. As they strolled about the long room, he asked about her thoughts on various subjects.

It seemed they enjoyed some of the same authors, though Darby was not fond of poetry. His favorite color was blue, not fashionable he knew, but one couldn't help that. He relished a good boxing match, she liked to fish, and they both enjoyed horseback riding. He loved the city, she loved the country, and neither could bring the other to change their opinion.

"Do you have a favorite vegetable?" Darby asked, a mischievous glint in his eye. "I'll tell you I only eat them drowned in butter."

"Oh my, what a waste of a good vegetable. I do not have a preference, but I hate cardoons and only tolerate broccoli." She giggled. "And what is your choice of dessert?"

"I'm not much for sweetmeats or that sort of thing. I prefer the sweetness of a female to that of a baked good."

"Flummery! I'm learning to see through you already." She laughed. "I saw you sneak a second chocolate tart last week at the Fenley's."

"I have been found out." He placed his hand over hers as they turned. "Christmas is coming upon us. Will you stay in Town or return to Pendleton Place?"

"I couldn't imagine not being home. And now with my sister-in-law Eliza and my young niece Althea, I wouldn't miss it. The caroling and mistletoe—"

"Mistletoe?" He stopped and turned to face her. "You have been caught under the ball?"

Those eyes, pinning her to the spot, shone with…need? Desire? "Why, yes. J-just chaste kisses, of course."

"Another first I would have liked to claim."

His gaze and words weakened her limbs, and when she thought her knees would give out, he turned and resumed their walk. What was she to think of that? Well, she could do the same.

"What traditions does your family have for the holiday?" she asked, thankful her voice was steady.

"I don't celebrate the day anymore. It has…" He paused then cleared his throat. "My mother and sister do the usual things, but my parents never enjoyed Christmas as some did."

"Oh, you should come to Pendleton Place. We celebrate from Christmas Eve until Twelfth Night. I wager I could change your mind." She'd seen the anguish in his eyes. Mattie had told her December was a melancholy month for her brother. Perhaps she could change that. If he did something out of the ordinary, like come to the country, he would have new memories for the month instead of focusing on the sad events of the past.

"I couldn't impose." He nodded to his sister, who waved from across the room. "I believe the whist game has come to an end."

"Do not change the subject," she insisted. "I believe some time in the country would be good for you. I know Nathaniel would welcome his good friend."

"I didn't mean to eavesdrop, but I must agree with Hannah," added Aunt Bertie. "You would be a welcome addition, indeed. Or are you afraid you might enjoy yourself?"

Hannah laughed at the challenge. "The gauntlet has been thrown down."

"Well, in that case, I will consider it."

CHAPTER NINE

ONCE UPON A WINDOW©

"Why has government been instituted at all? Because the passions of man will not conform to the dictates of reason and justice without constraint."

— ALEXANDER HAMILTON

St. Giles
Mid-December 1819

icholas stepped from the hackney and gave a slight nod to Walters, waiting across the street. They continued along Oxford at a quick pace toward the Rat's Nest, past the last of the private residences and public houses, their yellow sandstone structures lit with the soft glimmer of candlelight through the window panes. Gin houses, for the working man or wayward gentleman, and slash houses, frequented by thieves and prostitutes, soon replaced the private homes and respectable public houses.

Tonight, Colvin had left his carriage, spoken with his hired thug, and continued on foot. Misgiving niggled at his chest; something was off. The louse was making it too easy. Besides the change in transportation, there was an urgency to his walk. He followed the duke at a discreet distance. Colvin's dark cape and beaver hat blended into the foggy night, his silver cane tip flashing occasionally in the night, a small blinking beacon in the haze that kept Nicholas's target in sight.

The street narrowed, and the small shops were dark now with the windows shuttered. The buildings began to crowd together, taller edifices leaning against each other or tilted over the filthy streets and alleys.

Women leaned against slimy walls, their wares spilling out of stained bodices, smiles of yellow or gapped teeth flashing him as he passed quickly by. A skeleton of a dog scratched at his ear, earning several kicks from a group of boys ambling down the street. A drunk stopped in front of him, tottered before catching his balance, then urinated against the door of a tobacco shop. He had entered St. Giles, a rookery, a slum.

"Good evenin' to ye, my fine fella. Buy me an ale, would ye, darlin'?" A young doxy approached him, her eyes much too old for her years, her face creased with hard living.

"If I didn't have an appointment, I might consider it, ma'am," he responded with a nod, never altering his stride. A fit of giggles followed him as he turned a corner, keeping track of the dark figure ahead.

A pig emerged from a darkened alley and snuffled along the edge of the street, poking its nose in a murky puddle for anything edible. Darby pulled his scruffy brown hat low over his forehead. He doubted he would be recognized in this part of town but wouldn't take the chance. He passed a cluster of men singing drunkenly in front of gaming hells, more lady-birds strutting in front of would-be customers, their jackets open to reveal their merchandise. Glancing over his shoulder, he checked to see that Walters kept pace with him.

The stench of human waste, rotting food, and unwashed bodies increased, and Nicholas tucked his nose against his collar. Colvin turned into an alley. The footpad, keeping a distance in front of the duke, stopped at a back entrance. He spoke with someone, then approached the duke, and they both entered the slash house.

"My lord, do you wish me to go in?"

"Yes, Walters. It's his fourth haunt in a month, so he must be looking for something in particular."

The Bow Street runners often frequented these places, keeping up with informants and abreast of what was happening in the rookeries. Many establishments like these were also pawnshops and secretly fenced stolen goods. Walters had discovered the duke's routine through one of his old contacts. Colvin would enter a house, ask for a private room, and "interview" young boys. Walters also learned that this certain establishment had purchased several new lads this week from an orphanage outside London.

"Yes, my lord. He sits at a table and sips his ale while they remove their shirt. He looks them over like livestock at an auction and asks them questions."

"What sort of questions?"

"Don't know. He speaks softly and the boys usually nod or shake their head. I do know that any boys with scars or recent marks from beatings are sent away immediately."

"He wants them untouched, to be the first to inflict whatever torture he's disposed to administer." Bile rose in the earl's throat. "It's not about sex anymore. It's about pain and control."

Walters squinted through the fog over Nicholas's shoulder. "Mind yourself, sir. Some blokes are coming this way."

The men in homespun coats continued by, shoulders

hunched against the cold, hurrying home or to a warm tavern. The rookeries were also full of the wretched poor. Families that could afford nothing else, scraping by each week to pay the rent and feed their children. There were more families than criminals in the slums, but one still had to keep his wits about him.

Walters went inside, and Nicholas hunkered down, pulled up the collar of his worn coat, and tucked his face inside against the cold. His mind wandered to Hannah, those toffee-colored eyes, bits of gold flashing when she was challenged or the afternoon sun hit her face just right. He was beginning to look forward to their chats, wondering what she did when he was not with her, missing her smile, her laughter.

A splash behind him, a foot encountering a puddle, but he'd been distracted and turned too slowly to avoid the arm that now tightened around his neck. As he grasped the attacker's fingers and tried to flip him over, the *click* of a pistol made him freeze.

"That's better. No use both of us gettin' hurt, is there?"

The rancid breath of his assailant was moist against his cheek. Stale sweat, tobacco, and old fish mixed together. Nicholas struggled not to gag.

"I'm to deliver a message, word for word, from my *patron*." He chuckled and tightened his hold. "After that, I got me permission to have some fun with ye before I make my departure."

"Get on with it," Nicholas growled. He knew better than to let down his guard. It was his own fault that he was in this position. His fists curled, longing for retribution.

"I'm to tell ye to take care. Ye don't want the pretty little country girl to have the same fate as yer wife. But he wouldn't mind a taste of it on a tedious night."

Fury shot through Nicholas's veins. He slammed his head

back, the *crack* of skull against skull echoing against the damp walls of the alley. He turned, blinking back the pain, and the footpad stumbled backward. Nicholas made a fist and let loose, the frustration and fury finding release.

Satisfaction rippled through him as his knuckles connected with the man's jaw. The thug was a brute, holding steady but unable to retaliate. On the third punch, the man teetered. Behind him, Walters appeared and brought the butt of his pistol down on the assailant's noggin. The lout crumpled to the ground, his pistol clattering onto the stones.

"Colvin's gone. I think *this* was his purpose tonight." Walters waved his pistol at the unconscious lump and bent to pick up the dropped weapon. "I thought the sound of a shot might bring too much attention. What did he want?"

"A warning to leave off the duke. I milled his canister well enough before you fibbed him." Nicholas grimaced as he looked at the unconscious, bleeding man and shook his stinging hand. "Not that I'm complaining, mind you."

"I don't think we should linger here, my lord. Let's continue this conversation elsewhere." He grinned as he looked over his shoulder, slid the weapon into its holster, and made his way out of the alley. "Preferably an establishment with decent ale."

They left the stink of the alley and bypassed the unmoving form and other piles of refuse along the way. Retracing their steps, Nicholas bid Walters join him in the hackney. He pulled out a flask and handed it to the ex-runner, who sat back and pulled his cap from his unruly brown curls.

"He knows he's being followed?" He tipped the flask and took a long pull.

Nicholas nodded. "I was at Almack's last week—"

"Almack's? Beg pardon, my lord, but I can't see you going

there of your own free will." He took another swallow and handed back the silver flask.

"My sister is out this season. I'm committed to oversee her admirers, so it is somewhat against my will. But I digress," the earl admitted. "He approached my sister and another young lady who is presently under my protection. He has threatened to pursue his old habits with gently bred ladies if I continue my quest."

Walters let out a whistle. "A noxious leech, ain't he?"

Nicholas nodded again. "I need to proceed with more caution. I want to avoid any innocent victims, but I cannot give up. This pustule on humanity must be stopped. Any suggestions?"

"Aye, and aye. First off, leave the rookery to me. If I set a new man on him, he may think he's scared you off." Walters chuckled. "He's just arrogant enough to believe it."

"While I hate leaving all the dirty work to you, it may be the safest plan to keep the ladies out of danger."

"We're making him nervous if he's resorting to threats. Good sign, I think." The cab rolled to a stop in front of the Guinea, and Walters stepped out.

"Thank you for your help. You have been indispensable." Nicholas paused.

"Think nothing of it, my lord. I'll keep in touch in the usual fashion."

CHAPTER TEN

"Women are armed with fans as men with swords, and sometime do more execution with them..."

— ESSAY FROM *THE SPECTATOR* BY JOSEPH
ADDISON

Third week of December 1819

*H*annah snapped her fan open, trying to create a breeze in the stifling heat of the room. So this was a *crush*. Bodies crammed into room after room with barely space to turn around. No one could possibly enjoy this kind of party. She searched the crowd for Mattie and her aunt to tell them she needed air.

An enormous turquoise feather rippled above the dozens of heads. *There she is.* Making her way through the throng, she found Aunt Bertie and told her she would be outside in the garden. A group had made its way out there earlier, and the baron's daughter had been in the set.

As she reached the terrace, the crisp winter air cooled her

damp skin. Hannah took in a deep breath and descended the steps, looking for her friend and acquaintances. The garden had nicely laid-out paths, and she found herself walking under a full moon. The black sky, the huge round orb glowing white, and the fresh air away from the press of bodies made her sigh with contentment. She pulled her shawl more tightly around her.

"I take it you weren't impressed with the assemblage of titles inside."

She turned to find Lord Darby behind her, bang up to the mark in his gray and white striped waistcoat and matching dark gray coat and trousers. His blond hair shone almost white in the moonlight. He was smiling, and she wanted to kiss the dimple in his cheek.

Stop it! Why would kissing him cross her mind? Hannah beat down the wings in her stomach as he held out his arm.

"Would you care to stroll with me? I'm in no hurry to return to the mob either."

With a giggle, she took his arm. The now-familiar warmth rushed through her. Spying the scraped and bruised knuckles, she asked, "What happened? It looks painful."

"Oh, just a boxing mishap."

"You should always wear gloves," she admonished before looking at the flickering stars and letting out a long breath. "I'm used to our country estate. The last time I saw so many bodies penned up was shearing season."

"Sheep? I do see the resemblance."

Hannah laughed. "You realize we share the same wicked humor."

"It's one of your most endearing qualities."

"You flatter me, my lord." Her fingers clutched one end of her shawl that threatened to slip off her shoulders.

"I'm surprised you're out alone. While Lady Roberta is not one to follow propriety, I can't see her allowing you a stroll alone under the moonlight." He gripped her hand a little tighter.

The tone held a hint of reprimand, which surprised her. "I didn't think you were one to worry about the rules of society either, my lord." She looked up at his profile, the straight nose, strong jaw, square chin. He was magnificent, and her heart raced at their proximity and isolated surroundings. "I saw a group coming out for air and thought to join them. However, it seems they've been swallowed up by the night."

"My apology, Miss Pendleton, I overstepped. You have become dear to my sister, and because of that, dear to me. I tend to be protective of her, so I fear it has spilled over on to you." He stopped at the end of a path and turned to her.

Her pulse raced. With each evening and afternoon spent with him, each conversation, each shared look across the room, her heart had opened a little more to this man. She longed to wipe the haunted look from those riveting eyes. His face was the last image in her head at night and one of her first thoughts when she woke. She was smitten and no longer afraid to admit it.

Her brother was wrong about Lord Darby. He did want love; he just didn't realize it yet. But she would be waiting for him when he did. They were compatible in so many ways, and he stimulated her mind and… A boldness, likely from the champagne, claimed her.

"Your only affection toward me is because of your sister?" Hannah held his gaze, not allowing him to look away. She also held her breath as she waited for his reply.

He opened his mouth, closed it, and then shook his head. "No, you have crept into my affections on your own merit." His finger moved up and pushed a ringlet from her temple.

The light touch sent a ripple through her, and she found it hard to breathe.

"But I'm not a fit match for you, and I never will be.

I'm…" Darby looked up at the inky sky, clearly struggling to find words.

Compassion overtook reserve. She laid her hand on his cheek, her eyes misty as he closed his own. A sigh escaped him, blowing gently against her face.

"Nicholas," she said softly, "I see the man inside of you. He's a good man, a worthy man. And I won't give up on him."

He leaned into her palm. Her other hand cradled the other cheek, causing her shawl to slip from her shoulders and fall to the ground. A shiver ran through her, from the touch or the night air, she knew not. But in that moment, Hannah knew she loved this man.

He pulled her into his arms, his face buried against her neck. She breathed in the musky male scent of him, absorbed his warmth, and clung to his neck. Nicholas pulled back, staring down into her eyes. She felt as if he'd devoured her with a look, and it left her wanting more.

His head dipped, his lips lightly brushing hers, velvet pleasure sending lightning bolts through her core. She gasped when his tongue traced her lower lip, then dove inside her mouth. He tasted of brandy and lemon, and Hannah thought she would die from the sweet intimacy of it. She leaned into him, no longer trusting her legs to hold her steady, and his grip around her waist tightened.

Nicholas moaned, a sound that made her smile against his kiss. He tried to push away, but she pulled his head back down, feeling the exact moment he gave in. His shoulders relaxed and his hands began to roam, claiming her lips with urgency, demanding and passionate.

As he feathered her neck with kisses, her hand lingered on his sleeve, and the bunched muscles flexed beneath her touch. Her palm moved against his solid chest, and when he pressed his full length against her, she felt the hardness of him. He desired her as much as she desired him.

"By Christ, we can't do this," he growled into her hair. "You deserve better than a warped soul. I'll only hurt you."

"It's too late, so you're damned if you do and you're damned if you do not." She traced the cleft in his chin. Oh, how she'd longed to do that for weeks. Standing on tiptoe, she replaced her finger with her lips. "I suggest you kiss me again if you care for me at all."

With a groan, his mouth pressed against hers. His hands stroked her bare shoulders, running down her spine and back up to cup her face. His tongue requested entrance, and she willingly obliged. Hannah was dizzy, her stomach in flight, her limbs like a warm Sunday pudding.

This was what she had dreamed of since she was five years old. She'd had the face wrong, but it was the same blissful feeling she'd imagined. Everything about this kiss was right and good. It was not a mistake, and she would not let Nicholas sacrifice himself to guilt, not when it meant both their happiness.

Emotions raged in his chest. Pleasure, guilt, caution...fear. He was a fractured man, and Hannah needed someone who was not afraid to love. Being alone in this garden not only endangered her reputation, but endangered her life if Colvin had any of his spying thugs about. Yet he could not drag himself away, torturing his senses with her velvety skin, petal-soft hair, and delicious scent of apricot and citrus. A ragged moan escaped from deep in his chest, and he tried to step away, only to be pulled back down into the waters of temptation. Her fingers trailed his neck, and his control fled, lost in the essence of all things Hannah.

Nicholas knew the taste of her would haunt him that night, perhaps forever. In the back of his mind, he heard voices. An interruption to their tryst. "By Christ, we can't do this." He could hear the rasp in his voice. "You deserve better than a warped soul. I'll only hurt you."

Hannah said something clever, but it was lost on him as her eyes held his, seeing the genuine affection, her gaze willing him to admit his own. She placed a finger on his chin and drew it lazily down the crease, then leaned up and kissed the dent. Lust licked at his insides, his body a traitor as he tried to deny his reaction to her once more.

"I suggest you kiss me again if you care for me at all." Her voice, smooth and sultry, made his blood boil.

He held her face in his hands, her tawny eyes daring him, and he gave in. Gave in to her taunts, gave in to his desire, gave in to his heart. He loved Miss Hannah Pendleton, and it scared the hell out of him. But as their kiss deepened, an odd awareness washed over him. A sense of belonging, as if he were exactly where he was supposed to be. The comfort in that feeling, in her presence, was overwhelming.

The voices grew louder, and with a ragged breath, he stepped away from her. Her chest rose and fell, the creamy mounds beckoning for his touch. Nicholas swore under his breath and stooped to collect her shawl, arranging it around her shoulders and tugging her honeyed curls into some semblance of order. The actions calmed his nerves and gave him time to get his desire under control. He tucked her hand over his arm, and they moved silently toward the voices.

"Ah, there you are," called Lady Roberta as she turned a corner, Mattie on her heels. "We've been looking for you. I'm ready to take my leave. It's monstrous crowded, and the air is stifling."

"Yes, Aunt Bertie," Hannah said in a breathless tone. "Whatever you think is best."

"Good evening, Lord Darby," Lady Roberta said with a sly

smile. "I wondered where you'd got off to. I'm so glad my niece found someone to walk with."

"Happy to oblige, ma'am." He bowed slightly and turned to his sister. "Would you like to depart as well?"

"Oh, yes, I'm done to a thumb." Mattie gave him an odd look. "Are you feeling well? You look flushed. I hope you aren't coming down with whatever Mama has."

"It's probably just the nips of brandy from my flask and the brisk air." He avoided meeting Hannah's eyes. "Shall I call for the coach, then?"

They walked back, following Lady Roberta and his sister. "Would it be presumptuous to call you Hannah in private?" he asked in a whisper, head bent toward her. "And for you to call me Nicholas?"

"I believe I have already," she said, an impish light in her eyes. The moonlight cast golden highlights on her soft brown waves, and he wished they were alone again. "Will you attend the masquerade ball?"

"Will you?"

She nodded. "With the usual entourage, including your sister."

"Then I wouldn't miss it."

After escorting the ladies back to their townhouse, Nicholas eyed Mattie from across the carriage. He leaned back against the soft squab. "What's on your mind? I can see the words ready to spew from your mouth."

She laughed. "I was right. You like her."

He closed his lids, enjoying the sway of the carriage, feeling sleep coming on without the aid of brandy. "Yes, sweet sister, I like her. Very much." He opened his eyes to slits. "But do not read too much into it."

"Just knowing you may open your heart again is enough. I

will not push. Fate has its own direction, you know." But her smile held hope. So much hope. For a sister-in-law, he knew, and for her brother to find peace.

For the first time in years, Nicholas fell asleep in the month of December without drinking himself into a stupor. And for the first time in years, he felt the hole in his chest begin to close. Miss Hannah Pendleton, it seemed, was the missing piece in the puzzle of his heart.

CHAPTER ELEVEN

ONCE UPON A WIDOW©

"Sometimes the truth is found out too late to apply it to any effectual remedy."

— WILLIAM LAMB, SECOND VISCOUNT
MELBOURNE

*H*annah could not wipe the smile from her face. Instead, she tried to appear interested in the slice of cold meat pie her aunt had plopped onto her plate. They were having a cold repast before retiring, and Aunt Bertie's gaze held too many questions.

"You can say what you want, child, but I know when a woman's been kissed. And you my dear, have been thoroughly so." She beamed. "I realize I was amiss, giving you the opportunity to be alone, but when I saw him follow you out…"

"He followed me outside?" Hannah could feel the heat

spreading across her cheeks. "I thought he'd come across me by accident."

Aunt Bertie chuckled. "I don't believe there are accidents when it comes to love or fate. *Are* you in love with him?"

"I barely know him," she scoffed, trying to change the subject. "Did the costumes arrive for the masquerade?"

"Don't avoid the question. Time and love do not go hand in hand, child. One might be with a man for years and never find love with him, or it could happen in a day and one single look." Aunt Bertie popped the last bite of Wiltshire cheese into her mouth. "It only took one glance with Chester."

Hannah concentrated on the meat pie again. Could she tell her aunt? What if Lord Dar—Nicholas never mentioned the kiss again? What if he decided he couldn't give his heart again? He must have been deeply in love with his wife to continue holding a torch for five years. How could she compete with a dead woman?

"I'm waiting, my dear."

With a sigh, she nodded. "Yes, he kissed me. And then I kissed him." Her resolve fled, and Hannah launched into a full summary. "Oh, Aunt Bertie. It was just like Eliza said it would be. His touch, his smell, it was all so wonderful."

"You *are* in love with him." Aunt Bertie chortled. "Lud, but this is all working out devilish well."

Hannah gave a snort and dug into her pie now with gusto. She was suddenly ravenous.

"Are you ready?" called Aunt Bertie from the stairs. "The coach is waiting."

Eleanor of Aquitaine descended, her mask hanging from her wrist, bumping against her reticule. Hannah had chosen a festive, bottle-green velvet dress of medieval style with an underskirt of black silk. A string of holly and mistletoe was embroidered across the dark hem and along the black lace armbands, cuffs, and neckline. The bodice hugged her figure and exposed more of her breasts than she was accustomed. A black velvet rope twisted with diamonds adorned the drop waist. Her hair hung loose; the braided plaits encircling her head interspersed with more paste diamonds and emeralds. She took in Aunt Bertie's costume.

"Oh, Aunt, that color is lovely on you. I thought it was indigo until the light shone on it, and now it looks deep violet. And where did you get that scarf?"

"It's called Mazurine blue, and I brought the sari and scarf back from India with me. I love the print and the colors." She did a circle to show off the entire pattern of tiny birds of paradise, the silk dress changing from indigo to dark violet as the light played against it. The scarf lay over her head and draped down her shoulders and back. Gold bangles jingled at her wrists, and a thick gold braid wrapped around her throat. "It has such special memories."

"I do believe those walks are making you thinner. You look positively stunning!"

"Oh, pish! It's only the dress." But she beamed at her niece, obviously pleased someone had noticed. "Now, the bachelors will be lining up to dance with you. Remember, no more than two dances with Lord Darby or the tongues will wag."

"Yes, ma'am, I'll remember." Hannah sighed. "It's our last event before returning home for Christmas. I can't believe a month has passed so quickly."

"Will Lord Darby come, do you think?"

She shook her head. "I have no idea. We'll see what tonight brings."

.   .   .

The masquerade was at a marquess' townhouse on the Strand. Lights blazed as they pulled in front of the brick exterior, footmen waiting to open the doors for guests. It was a formal affair, except the guests were not announced since it was a masquerade. Three gaslit chandeliers dropped from the ceiling, turning gowns, jewels, masks, canes, and fobs into a dazzling array of glitter and pomp. It made Hannah's head spin. They ascended the circular staircase to the ball-room, stopping at least twice as Aunt Bertie spoke with this person or that, introducing them as Eleanor and Aditi.

"What is Mattie wearing?" Aunt Bertie asked.

"She has a traditional Venetian costume, so look for a hooded black cape."

"Welcome, my ladies," said a female in a terrible Italian accent, "I am a stranger here in England and in need of friends."

Hannah would know her friend's smile anywhere. She was lovely in a coquelicot gown with white poppies embroidered in stripes down the full red skirt. The color brought out the pink of her cheeks, and the black hood covered her jonquil locks. Her mask was red with a border of black paste diamonds, and it made her light blue eyes stand out against the darker color.

"Oh, Hannah, I'm so forlorn this is our last get-together before you go." She clasped her friend's hand. "You look stunning!"

"Thank you," Hannah said, adjusting her own black mask beaded with tiny green paste beads. "I'll return in a month. Can you believe that's how long we've known each other?"

"You'd think you girls have been friends since childhood," added Aunt Bertie. "How did you know it was us, my dear? Are we so apparent?"

Mattie laughed. "Well, I've already seen Hannah's costume, and you said you would wear something from your travels. And as I got closer, I could hear your voice. It is quite distinct, Lady Roberta."

The older woman chuckled. "Well played! Now, let's mingle and see who is who, shall we?"

The masquerade was the most spectacular event Hannah had ever witnessed. Several guests were dressed as pirates, one with his shirt slightly open, causing stares and giggles from the ladies. Others were sultans, with huge turbans wrapped around their heads. She saw at least two wizards, several monks, bishops, peasants, and one Queen Elizabeth. Another woman dressed as a concubine, her flimsy turquoise pantaloons hugging her ankles and waist with an equally sheer material covering her arms. Her red hair hung loose with a riot of curls framing her face, and an opaque veil covered her features.

"Why does that sailor look so…feminine, and that queen so…uncomely?" Hannah asked, her brows drawn together as she studied some of the costumes more closely.

"Oh, my dear, I forgot this is your first masquerade. Women dress as men, men dress as women. All the more difficult to decipher who is behind the mask. It is monstrous funny, is it not?"

"Nicholas is here somewhere. He said he had some business to attend to." Mattie searched the room. "I pointed you both out to him when you entered. He said to give you his regards, and he'll join us shortly."

Hannah's stomach dropped. He'd seen them enter and not come forward to meet them. Mattie's arm through hers proved Hannah's dismal failure at hiding her disappointment. "If you could have seen his face when he saw you at the top of the stairs. His mouth fell open."

Aunt Bertie grinned. "Of course it did. And I'm sure you've dropped a few jaws yourself this evening, Lady Matilda. Shall we find some refreshments?"

An hour later, a deep rich voice whispered in her ear. "You are the stuff of dreams, *la mia bella signorina.* Shall I take the first dance or save the best for last?"

She turned, her skirt brushing across black buckled shoes and satin azure knee breeches that hugged his muscular thighs. Hannah immediately recognized Nicholas's piercing blue eyes. A white shirt with ruffles at the throat and sleeves was covered by a long gold satin coat. He wore a brown wig, pulled back and tied in a short tail by a gold leather thong.

"May I introduce myself? I am Giacomo Casanova, newly cast out from my beloved Venice." He bowed and kissed her hand.

Hannah's breath caught, the touch of his lips against her bare skin shocking. Aunt Bertie had insisted on no gloves since it was not part of the medieval costume. "I am Eleanor, Queen consort of England and duchess of Aquitaine. Your reputation precedes you, sir."

"As does yours, Your Highness."

Another bow, another kiss to her knuckles, another shiver through her body.

A pirate approached and bowed to Mattie. "Madam, may I have the next dance?" He was handsome, with long deep brown hair and braids framing his face and twinkling hazel eyes. A worn leather tricorn hat crowned his head, a bandanna wrapped around his forehead, and a black patch over one eye. His costume fit across broad shoulders, and the snug pants disappeared into tall, cuffed leather boots.

She glanced at Nicholas and Hannah and then smiled. "Why, good sir, I cannot dance with a stranger, let alone a treacherous pirate. My brother would never allow it."

"I am John Rackham at your service, ma'am." He put his hand to the side of his mouth and whispered loudly, "Known to some as Calico Jack."

All three ladies gasped in mock horror, enjoying the theatrics.

"I've always wanted to dance with a pirate," Mattie answered. "But you must promise not to kidnap me, for I have to be home by dawn."

"I cannot vouch for my honesty, but chivalry is not dead, my lady." He held out his arm as the first notes of a quadrille began.

"If I am not back by the end of the set, send out the Royal Navy," called Mattie over her shoulder.

"My sister seems to have found her tongue along with the mask." Darby scowled at the retreating Venetian and pirate joining three couples. "I'm not sure I like it."

Hannah laughed. "She feels brave behind the mask. It will give her confidence."

"You have given her confidence, Miss Pendleton, er, Your Highness, and I thank you for it."

"Mattie has become a cherished friend. Do not offer gratitude when I do it for selfish reasons." Hannah was enjoying the banter, the conversation, the atmosphere until she looked at Nicholas.

His face had hardened and the smile vanished. "And would you mind sharing those selfish reasons?"

She cocked her head and studied him. A smile returned to her lips as she realized what he was about. "I always wanted a sister, my lord. Another girl close to my age to share secrets with, laugh and be silly with, be myself with. I feel Mattie and I are kindred souls. That is all I meant by it." She longed to reach up and touch his cheek, reassure this fragile earl that she was trustworthy.

"I am sorry. I... I do not trust easily." Regret flashed in his eyes and he bowed, taking her hand and kissing it again. When he looked up again, the heart-stopping grin was back and he winked. "I will find an opportunity to steal you away for a brief time tonight and make a better apology. Be awake on all suits for my signal."

"I adore a bit of danger, Signor Casanova." Her eyes shone with amusement. "I do hope you live up to your name."

Two sets later, Hannah shared refreshments with her aunt and Mattie. A highwayman approached, bumped into Hannah, and slid a paper against her palm. He murmured apologies and walked away.

"How rude," exclaimed Aunt Bertie. "I swear he did that on purpose."

"Are you all right, Hannah?" asked Mattie. "That was quite a jostle."

She nodded. "I'm fine. However, I need to tend to necessities. If you'll excuse me?"

Hannah weaved through the crowd to the hallway and found a private alcove. She unfolded the parchment and read the note.

Meet me below at half past eleven. Back stairs, end of hall, door will be open. C~

Casanova. She pressed her lips together, pushing down the excitement from Nicholas's note. A secret tryst. Was this why masquerade balls were all the crack? Making her way back to the ballroom, she checked the time. Half an hour. Not enough time to join the next dance set.

While Hannah chatted with several guests, the time moved at a snail's pace. With five minutes to spare, she slipped out of the party and found the back steps. The narrow staircase was dark, and she kept her hands on the wall as she moved carefully toward the shadowy hallway.

Hannah neared the end of the passage and found a door slightly ajar. She poked her head in and called out, "Hello?" No answer. Pushing the door open wider, she stepped into the darkened room. *Slam!* The heavy wood reverberated in its frame. A hand gripped her arm and pushed her against a wall. It was pitch black, and she could see nothing. She hugged herself and rubbed her arms as goosebumps rose on her skin.

"Nicholas," she whispered in a shaky voice. "Please, you know I hate the dark." Feeling along the wall, she moved back in the direction of the door.

A soft chuckle behind had her spinning the opposite way. She clung to the wall, afraid to move into the empty abyss. Why was he doing this? Did he think this was a game she enjoyed?

"Do you remember when we played Twirl the Trencher, and losers had to share a secret? Mine was that I am afraid of the dark. Please, don't tease. It frightens me."

A whisper sent warm breath feathering her cheek. "Don't excite me, my pet, I feed on fear." Then the presence was gone. But the faint odor of leather and peppermint lingered. She'd smelled that combination before.

Oh sweet Mary, he's not Nicholas.

"Who are you? Where is Lord Darby?" The growing panic, thick in her throat, made it difficult to get words out.

A hand gripped her shoulder, pain shooting down her arm, and something trailed up her cheek. "You smell divine, my dear." He breathed deeply and moaned. "You are untouched, I'm sure of it."

Hannah opened her mouth to scream, but no sound came out. *Oh God, oh dear God!* She clutched her belly, shaking her head back and forth. Gulping air, she tried to calm herself.

She straightened and, with both hands against the wall, tried to inch along rough stone. The friction against her skin brought some coherence to her thoughts, and she concentrated on the texture as she moved. This must be some sort of cellar, for storage of some kind. If she could find something to protect herself with.

"Oh, let's not be in a rush, eh? I doubt anyone will notice you missing until the unmasking at midnight," he whispered. "Plenty of time for what I have in mind."

Hannah forced herself to breathe. What had her brother taught her to do if she were ever cornered by a frisky boy? Her mind was blank. *Think!*

Fwoosh! A match cast an eerie yellow light about the room. A man in a cape and mask, his face shadowed but the dark hair and eyes glittered. Then he shook out the weak glow.

A light touch against her hair, like something was crawling… Warm breath against her cheek. The cave came back to her, the blind terror, the spider in her hair. Hannah began flapping her arms around her head, slapping at whatever was in her hair. Someone was screaming hysterically, and somewhere in the back of her mind, she realized it was her.

Fwoosh! The man again, his smile oddly grotesque in its brightness. "Now you see me." He shook out the light. "Now you don't."

The chuckle gave Hannah a clue to the direction he was coming from. She sucked in air, let it out slowly, as her mother had taught her when panic overtook her as a child. It helped, and she hugged her stomach as her long locks were lifted, warm breath now on the back of her neck. She whirled and pushed as hard as she could.

Hands grabbed her arms as her brother's words came back to her. *A well-placed knee will give you a good five minutes.* She could feel his face close to hers and tried not to gag. She jerked her knee up as hard as she could and flinched as she made contact.

Her attacker howled with pain, and she heard him drop to the floor. "You little bitch, you'll pay for that." He wasn't whispering anymore.

Hannah began to scream again as loud as she could, then fumbled along the wall for the door, a knob, escape. Her hand hit something hard and protruding. She sobbed in relief, fumbling with it, pulling, rattling, and screaming again for help. The hem of her dress caught on something, and she pulled.

"Get. Over. Here. Now." The voice behind her was cold with rage. He yanked hard on her skirt, pulling her off balance. She fell onto her back, her head hitting the stone floor. She blinked and saw spots floating before her eyes. The smell of leather and peppermint was next to her again, and she remembered.

The Duke of Colvin.

"Let's see what Darby has taught you, hmm?" he snarled. "I know you've kissed him. It was quite a show in the garden." His thumb pressed against her throat. "I believe you'll find my attentions a bit more…demanding."

Hannah gasped and tried to suck in a breath. Her hands searched along the floor for anything solid and latched onto a smooth piece of broken pottery. She found the edge, wrapped her fingers around it, striking blindly with all her strength.

"Aaaagh!" His grip relaxed, and he sat up. His weight pushed the air from her belly for a moment. "You have spirit, I'll give you that. But I've had worse than that for a paid pleasure."

Colvin grabbed a handful of her hair and shook her. Her head pounded as if it would explode. She began to scream again, hoping for someone, anyone to hear her. A hand covered her mouth, and she sank her teeth into the flesh. He released her with a yelp, and she took a breath, letting out another scream.

"You bloody whore," he howled and then let out a ghastly chuckle. "I'll enjoy bringing you down. The look on Darby's face when he finds—"

The door rattled. "Hannah!"

She began to fight with all the strength left, pummeling and kicking until the duke rolled off with a curse. "Nicholas!"

Two heavy thumps against the door were followed by splintering wood, then weak light flooded the enclosure. Two figures rushed in as she rolled over on to her hands and knees, gasping for breath, tears streaming down her cheeks. Then Nicholas was there, cradling her in his arms, rocking her, whispering soothing words. She clung to him, her body trembling as she gulped in air.

CHAPTER TWELVE

"Justice is the insurance which we have on our lives and property. Obedience is the premium which we pay for it."

— WILLIAM PENN

December 22, 1819

"Get up you blaggard, in the name of the King," demanded a voice Hannah did not recognize.

"I'm afraid you don't realize who you are addressing." Colvin sounded revoltingly assured. "I'm afraid our tryst got a little out of hand, but she did meet me willingly."

"NO!" Hannah rasped, "You tricked me with a note. I thought it was from…" How could she admit she was meeting Nicholas here alone? She would be ruined, whichever story came out. And when he set her off his lap and stood, turning his back on her, she knew Nicholas had come to the same conclusion. She swiped the renewed tears from her cheeks.

"I'm afraid she's embarrassed," he continued. "She needn't worry about her reputation. I suppose I could marry the chit. I do need an heir—"

Crack!

Hannah looked up as Colvin's head snapped back. First one fist then another plunged into the duke's stomach, producing a painful grunt and gasp. Nicholas quickly followed it with another upper to the jaw, and Colvin crumpled to the floor, his head making a sickening thump against the flagstone. Nicholas straddled the man and punched him again, and again, and again.

"Darby! If you kill him, we can't hang him."

Nicholas let his arms drop to his sides, his chest heaving as he looked down at the bloody duke. "I'd prefer to do it myself," he argued, wiping the sweat from his face with his coat sleeve.

The duke turned his head to the side and spit. A vile laughter faded into a bout of wheezing. "Look at the note. It's signed with a "C" for Colvin." He spit again and drew in a harsh breath. "She met me willingly. And even if she didn't, I would never hang for rape. I am the sixth Duke of Colvin and my father served the king well."

"I thought it was 'C' for Casanova." Hannah's voice was no more than a croak. "He trapped me in here, i-in the dark."

"Tell that to a jury of *my* peers." Colvin tried to push Nicholas off, let out a low moan, and fell back against the flagstone. "No matter what you accuse me of, I'll cry off with privilege of peerage."

Two uniformed men appeared at the door. Nicholas stood and rubbed his palms on the front of his costume, as if wiping the stink of the man from his body. He turned and walked to Hannah, holding out his hand. She reached up and he pulled her to her feet. Her knees refused to obey, so she leaned against him to gain her balance. In less than a heartbeat, he had scooped her into his arms. He buried his face in her hair.

"I am so sorry, my love, so sorry. He will never hurt you again. No one will ever hurt you again." He nodded toward the door. "I need to get Miss Pendleton out of his sight and see to any injuries."

Hannah wrapped her arms around his neck and tucked her head under his chin. Tears soaked her face and neck and her insides quaked like jelly. She could hear the duke's rants, her stomach twisting as she remembered his touch.

"Do not touch me, you blasted imbeciles. I am a Peer of the Realm! I am above this, I say," yelled the duke, then coughed and spat more blood.

The men ignored his tirade and jerked him to his feet.

"I'm afraid your privileges do not extend to treason, my lord. I'm sure your father who, as you pointed out, was a loyal subject of the king, would agree. I suggest, if you wish to retain any dignity, you should come with us quietly."

"Who the bloody hell are you?" he asked, the first tinge of fear coating his words. "I demand to speak to someone with authority."

"That would be me, Lord Chester Hatford. I am a representative of the Home Office and the Crown. We have been watching you, Your Grace. It seems you have interesting friends who ask you for money." Lord Chester placed himself in front of the battered duke. "Unfortunately, it's those investments which seem to have caused the Crown some anxiety."

"There has been some mistake. You have no proof of wrongdoing."

"Ah, but we have or I would never presume to put you, *the Duke of Colvin*, under arrest. I'm afraid your visits to Caro Street have been documented, along with your funding of the Spencean Philanthropists." He shook his finger at the duke. "Your Grace, consorting with factions who wish to overthrow our government is treason. Shameful, really."

"I demand—"

"I am sorry, but you are not in a position to demand. Your only hope will be to share names. Names of those plotting to assassinate our cabinet, names of the conspirators who believe it is permissible to overthrow our government. Perhaps the Regent will reduce your hanging to a beheading." He gave a mirthless chuckle. "I've been told it's much quicker and more humane. And I understand from your *friend* Lord Darby that you are quite the humanitarian."

The duke was half-escorted, half-dragged from the store-room. *Blast Hatford,* thought Nicholas, *he should have let me finish the whoreson.* He tightened his grip on Hannah when she moaned softly. As Lord Chester followed them, Lady Roberta's voice boomed from the hall. "Hannah! Where is my niece?" she demanded, though panic sounded in her voice.

"In here, ma'am. Not to worry, she's safe," called Nicholas, then to Hannah, "Sorry, my sweet, I hope that didn't hurt your head."

"No," she whispered. "Just don't let me go."

"Never!" He kissed her forehead. "Let's get you upstairs and find a doctor. Your skull has quite a lump."

He said a silent prayer to God, to Lord Chester, and to Walters. It turned out those two men were acquainted. Hatford had contacted the Bow Street runner, looking for some information. The intelligence had led Walters to one of Colvin's men. The men had sent a message to Darby, and they'd met tonight under cover of the masquerade.

The terror in his chest when he'd realized both Colvin and Hannah were missing had been worse than... Worse than that night five years ago. Nicholas kissed the top of her head again. No, he would never let her go.

"You saved me. He almost, he almost…"

"Shhh, you were so brave, my sweet, so brave." He tightened his hold on her quivering form. "I don't think he expected such courage."

Lady Roberta intercepted the trio at the door. She bumped into Lord Chester and froze, silent for once.

"I beg your pardon, ma'am," he said and stepped to the side to let her pass.

"Chester!" exclaimed Aunt Bertie. "Merciful heavens, is that you?"

"Bertie?" Hatford asked. "My Bertie from Calcutta?"

"How do you know Lady Roberta?" asked Nicholas.

The older woman squealed, her hands on both cheeks. "Oh, what a surprise. What are you doing here?"

"I'm doing a bit of work for the Home Office. Now, let me look at you." He placed his hands on her shoulders and smiled. "I was hoping our paths would cross while I was in London, though not under these circumstances. May I call on you tomorrow?"

Lady Roberta and Hatford led the way, chatting as if they'd just run into one another at Hyde Park. Walters met them in the dark upstairs hallway and ushered them out a servants' entrance to a waiting coach. Nicholas climbed in and settled Hannah on his lap, pulling a wool rug around her.

"The physician will be waiting at your house, my lord." He doffed his cap in apology. "I didn't know the lady's address but figured you'd want her seen to right away. In private."

"Thank you, Walters, for everything." Nicholas settled back against the squab. He took a deep breath and relaxed for the first time in hours. "Is that agreeable, Lady Roberta?"

"Of course, of course." She waved to Hatford before the

coach lurched forward. "I want to hear the entire story. Every detail."

"She has quite a concussion. Keep her quiet, no physical activity or travel for a week." The physician snapped his bag shut. "Give her the tea I prescribed to help her sleep, and I'll leave some laudanum."

"Thank you for coming so quickly." Nicholas blew out a long breath. "She's been unconscious since the ride home. I was afraid she might not wake up."

"She woke briefly. Lady Roberta will nurse her as well as I could for now, and I'll stop by daily to check on her." He paused. "I realize it's an imposition, but I think it best not to move the young lady."

"We are happy to have her here," said Mattie. "She will be disappointed to miss Christmas with her family, though."

"Good evening, then," said the doctor. "I'll see you tomorrow."

Mattie laid a hand on Nicholas's arm. "I sent word to the Pendleton townhouse and instructed the lady's maid to pack necessities and ride back in our carriage. Tomorrow Lady Roberta can arrange for whatever else they need."

"How are you holding up, dear sister? This has been quite an evening for all of us."

She smiled. "Fine, now that Hannah has been found and no fatal injuries incurred."

"I echo that sentiment."

"And how do you fare, dear brother? You were white as bleached linen when I saw you carrying her through the kitchens."

Nicholas ran a hand through his hair. "I admit I was unnerved." He laughed at her look. "Fine, I was terrified. It made me realize…"

"Yes?"

"How much I care for her."

Mattie beamed. "Oh, this will be a wonderful Christmas. We are decorating this year, and I don't care what you or Mama say. Our guests will expect a festive day!"

Nicholas closed his eyes and said another prayer. *Let this be the year I put her to rest. I put it all to rest.*

CHAPTER THIRTEEN

"Though the sex to which I belong is considered weak, you will nevertheless find me a rock that bends to no wind."

— ELIZABETH I

*D*ecember 24, 1819

"What do you mean, I can't help?" Hannah wagged a finger at her aunt. "I have helped decorate for Christmas every year since I could walk."

"I'll compromise. You can sit in the drawing room and help weave the greenery. But you need to rest." Aunt Bertie smirked. "I will not suffer the wrath of Darby if something happens. He's like a mother hen, clucking around you, rearranging your pillows, asking for the hundredth time if you'd like some tea."

"I do believe he wants me to float away on a sea of tea," Hannah agreed. Her smile was brilliant. "He's been so attentive. I'm getting quite spoiled."

"Get used to that," said Mattie, who entered with an

armful of pine. "Lady Roberta, did you have mince pies prepared for the holiday?"

"Of course, dear. Did your mother not have the cook do the same?"

Mattie shook her head. "We haven't celebrated much since… Do you suppose we might share?"

Hannah's heart went out to her friend. "Of course, we will be here anyway! And a word of warning, our family is quite traditional."

Aunt Bertie nodded. "Oh, we'll play games and eat and drink and make merry. It will be a monstrous good time, you'll see."

Hannah was glad to be among friends but still reeling from the masquerade. Her head was tender but she refused the laudanum. She was still in disbelief that the duke was being held for treason. It seemed poetic justice that the family who had been untouchable, that had cheated in cards and almost ruined one family, would now lose everything to the Crown. The thought of Colvin still made her shudder. It astonished her that he'd gone to such an extreme just to taunt Nicholas.

Nicholas, the man who had rescued her, who had hovered over her anxiously for two days, who had said he would never let her go. She vaguely remembered his words, being swept up in his arms, being carried up the stairs. She had felt so safe, surrounded by his strength, and had fallen asleep knowing she was secure in his care. Nicholas had kept vigil by her bed until she had woken. Aunt Bertie said the man couldn't be persuaded to leave her side. Yet, he'd made no proclamations of love.

"May I be of assistance, ladies?" asked Nicholas from the doorway. "Or should I retreat to the library while I can?"

"Help, please." Hannah patted the chair next to her. "You can help with the bough I'm making for the door."

"Mistletoe is involved, I hope?" He grinned, an impish smile deepening the cleft in his chin. "The task suddenly got more interesting."

"You are a rake, sir," Hannah scolded, "and I wouldn't have it any other way."

The afternoon passed quickly. The drawing room was soon filled with the smell of pine, and the servants had been given tasks to decorate the dining room, parlor, and staircase. The mince pies had been brought over, and Hannah's sheet music had arrived that morning.

"So did your family observe any Christmas traditions in the past?" she asked. Nicholas sat next to her, handing her pieces of ivy and mistletoe to lace into the pine boughs. "Mattie seems so excited about this celebration. She's almost as eager as a child herself."

The earl watched her fingers deftly weave a vine of ivy and then a clump of berries into the greenery. "Yes, long ago. We burned the Yule log, received gifts on St. Nicholas Day, and I remember my father always giving a special package to my mother on the New Year."

"It was a happier time." Hannah paused in her work. "I hope tomorrow will be a happier time for both of you."

"It already is, dear Hannah, it already is." He handed her another bunch of mistletoe. "I'm afraid I am the one who put the damper on this holiday. And my mother. I won't take all the blame."

Hannah longed to ask him about his wife, the circumstances, if he would be able to truly move on. But she hated to ruin the day and feared what his answer might be. What if she saw a tenderness in his eyes that he'd never shown to her? It would break her heart. She took the coward's path and said nothing.

"Where do you get your love for the holidays? Your brother enjoys this time of year but no more than the average person. I can't see your mother suddenly becoming jovial once a year."

"Ah, my aunt has kept the traditions going in our family. My paternal grandmother loved Christmas and all it entailed. We would spend the month with her in London, and Aunt Bertie always came. We'd help Cook make mince pies, practice the carols, decorate. All the things we'll be doing here, you see."

"I know mother won't deign us with her presence until tomorrow, but where is Lady Roberta?" asked Nicholas. "It seems so…so quiet without her."

"You are a cad," admonished Mattie, entering the room and engaging in the last part of the conversation. "She's at her townhouse gathering more necessities for their stay here."

"If I'm to be honest, I've grown quite fond of the woman."

"Well, doesn't that warm my buns and make my cheeks rosy," declared Aunt Bertie from the hall. "I have a feeling my niece had something to do with your sudden affection for this old woman."

Hannah and Mattie giggled at her unusual choice of words. Her aunt was a beaded reticule in a sea of stuffy pockets. A little over the top on occasion, but a more genuine and compassionate soul would be hard to find.

"Lady Roberta, I—"

"Oh, I know I can be quite a basketful. Pay me no heed, I'm just glad you came around."

That evening they played Alphabet Minute, laughing at the silly dialogue they created. Lady Darby joined them, feeling better now that her fever had left. She still looked wan but insisted she enjoyed the company. They retired early in anticipation of a full day on Christmas.

As she reached her room, Aunt Bertie stopped her.

"May I come in for a moment?" she asked, her face flushed.

"Of course, are you feeling fine? I hope you aren't catching what Lady Darby has."

"Oh no, child, quite the opposite. It's wonderful news." She put her hands to her cheeks and beamed. "Chester wants to court me again. He's been a widower now, you know, these past seven years. He said life is too short not to go after what you want. And I am still what he wants."

"Gracious," exclaimed Hannah, "he wants to marry you?"

"I assume that would follow courting." Her brown eyes sparkled with happiness. "He's been working for the Home Office since before the war. Can you imagine? My country squire chasing after spies!"

"So he enjoys adventure more than you thought?" Hannah hugged her aunt. She had a feeling Aunt Bertie had been lonelier than she cared to admit. Or perhaps she hadn't realized how lonely she was until she encountered Chester again.

"Oh Aunt, I'm so happy for you. He seems like a very nice man."

"Lud, am I too old to fall in love again?"

"You're one of the youngest people I know. And I don't believe you ever fell out of love. He was your one regret, remember?"

She nodded. "Well, I'll let you get some rest. You will meet him tomorrow. He's stopping by. Thank you for your ear, love."

As Hannah prepared for bed, she considered Aunt Bertie and her beau, but as she fell asleep, her thoughts turned to Nicholas. As they always did. The past two days had been like a dream, despite her aching head. His sincere affection had her daring to hope, yet something was not quite right.

What of his tragic wife? Why hadn't she the nerve to question him? She could have asked Mattie but it seemed an intrusion on his privacy.

Had the devotion he'd held for her faded enough? Could she take the place of the woman he'd continued to love for so many years? Mattie had shown her a portrait. Alice had been a beautiful, delicate woman. If they'd held each other so dear, why had she committed suicide? Perhaps she'd truly had a weak mind and suffered from melancholy. Or had the love been one-sided? If she'd been forced into marriage when she cared for another, how tragic that would have been for both of them.

Hannah woke late that night to a loud thump in the room next to hers. She lay still, wondering if it had been a dream. Another thump, then a crash, as if someone had fallen. Sweeping back the counterpane, she put on her robe and peeked into the hallway. A dim light shone from under the door. Incoherent mumbling accompanied the next thump, and she recognized Nicholas as he cursed.

She crept to the door and knocked softly. Silence. Perhaps he didn't want to be disturbed. *Then he shouldn't make so much noise.* As she turned away, the soft, terribly off-tune voice of Nicholas began singing.

"Angels we have heard on high," came the slurred words of the earl.

He was drunk! She'd heard that he would get foxed late at night during December, the memories all coming back to him. Mattie said that since Hannah had arrived, the drinking had slowed.

"Swwwwweetly sing-singing o'er the… o'er the… Bloody hell."

So much for Hannah's good influence. She pushed open the door and saw him standing in the middle of the room, weaving like a sapling in the wind, a bottle hanging from one hand.

"Hello, my ssssweet Hannah. Hhhelp me. I can't... I can't remember the blasted words."

To her dismay, she found he looked adorable. His face was open, no mask hiding his thoughts or feelings. He looked delighted to see her. His body staggered dangerously to one side and she rushed to him, putting his arm around her shoulders and removing the brandy from his hand.

"Trying to sssteal a drink for yourself, eh? Yyyyou sssly little vixen." He gave her a kiss on the mouth, a loud smack. He stilled, the smile fading from his lips. "I love you, Miss Hannah Pendleton." The words came out clear and sober. "You are mmmmy guardian angel." And the sodden Nicholas was back.

"Why don't we get you to the bed?" she asked and tried to move him toward the large four-poster bed. She was surprised when he dug in his heels.

"Nnnno, no, no. That's where she did it. That's why I nnnnever ssssleep here." He waved a wobbly hand at the bed, a paper crumpled in his fist. "I've come to say goodbye. She has been avvvenged!" With that, the earl sunk to the floor, fell back with a *thump* and promptly began to snore.

Hannah sank onto her haunches and brushed a blond lock from his forehead. The back of her finger lingered down his cheek. She leaned forward and kissed him softly on the mouth. "I love you too," she whispered.

He groaned and rolled over, his fist unclenching and the crumpled paper fell onto the carpet. She picked it up, curious eyes drawn to the feminine writing on the parchment. Her hand flew to her mouth as she realized it must be in Alice's handwriting, dated December 24. The night she died. Should she read it? But her gaze was already on the words, and she couldn't seem to tear her eyes away.

. . .

December 24, 1814

Nicholas,

Before I go, I must tell you how very sorry I am. I do not blame you for your outburst. You deserved so much better on your wedding night. A virgin, as every man dreams of. I wanted to tell you of the pregnancy, but Mama insisted it would all work out once we were married. In my heart, I knew better.

I was tricked into being alone with the man, and he had his way with me. When my family threatened to reveal his foul behavior, he laughed in our faces. He knew what I did not at the time. As a Peer of the Realm, I would not be a victim, but a woman trying to marry above her station. I will tell you his name, in the hopes of saving future innocents.

His father is the Duke of Colvin, you see. The son is a beast, and I fear his child will be a beast just like him. I realize now that neither of us would ever be happy, knowing the marriage began on a foundation of deceit. I cannot bring this child into the world. I cannot look into your eyes and see my betrayal reflected in them every day for the rest of my life. I am at peace with my decision. It will cause the least misery for all concerned. And I will be at rest. Finally at rest.

Please forgive me,

Alice

Tears streaked her cheeks as she read the final words of a

distraught woman. No, she had not been in her right mind. But she had done the deed with complete clarity. Hannah could neither blame her nor approve of her actions.

Nicholas stirred. "We did it, Alice. We got the bloody devil."

She brushed the hair back from his cheek. Nicholas. The man she loved. He'd been through so much, carried so much responsibility on his shoulders. The guilt he must bear for her death. The mission she laid upon him.

"Justice will be had." He rolled toward her lap. "How fitting he should hang."

Someone cleared their throat.

"Beg your pardon, my lady, but may I try to get him back to his rooms?" Nicholas's manservant stood at the door. "I do apologize. He usually stays put once he opens a bottle. I was having a bit of holiday spirits, and I—"

"A bloody tit for a bloody tat, by God!" the earl mumbled into Hannah's lap.

"No apology needed," Hannah said to the manservant hovering above them and wringing his hands. "Yes, let's see him to bed. I'm afraid it will take both of us."

CHAPTER FOURTEEN

"It is never too late to be what you might have been."

— GEORGE ELIOT

December 25, 1819

*N*icholas sat up, clutched his pounding temples, and lay back down against the soft mattress. The pillows cradled his aching head as he tried to remember how he got to bed. His mouth was dry and tasted like a combination of bad ale, good brandy, and rotten fish. If he lost his accounts, his stomach would feel better.

Don't fight it, he warned himself. He swung his feet over the bed, rose unsteadily, and then squatted down, holding on to the mattress. He fumbled for the chamber pot beneath and pulled it out just in time to fill it. Wiping his mouth on the sleeve of his nightshirt, he slowly made it back onto the bed. What was the last thing he remembered?

Drinking. Reading the letter as he always did, but for the last time. Then… Oh, God. He went to the room. He wanted to tell her they had done it. The duke would not hurt anyone else. And Nicholas would watch the scum hang. And swing.

A vague image of Hannah… Blast! What had he said? He couldn't remember any words, only her face smiling at him and then…nothing. Blast and damn!

His manservant knocked at the door.

"Come in."

"Good morning, my lord." He appeared by the bedside with a tray.

"Is it? I didn't sleep past breakfast?" That was a small miracle.

"No, sir. Lady Matilda wants to make sure you attend them in the dining room. It is Christmas Day, my lord."

"Yes, it usually follows Christmas Eve."

"This was also sent by my lady. It was prescribed by the physician."

"Physician? When did he see me?"

"He did not, my lord. Miss Pendleton told him you might be feeling a bit poorly."

Let's see him to bed. I'm afraid it will take both of us.

"She saw me in my…" Nicholas moaned.

"Condition? Yes, my lord." He handed the earl a murky liquid.

"If it helps, I'll try it." He tipped back his head and took the vile concoction in one gulp. "Gad! That's enough to make a man quit drinking."

"Yes, my lord."

Nicholas fidgeted with his cravat and ran a hand through his hair. He'd dressed for the day with a red-peony waistcoat and dark-gray coat over matching breeches. The day was cloudy and looked like snow. Perfect. That should fit right into his plans. Whatever the physician had sent him had worked. His head was no longer twice the size, and his stomach rumbled for breakfast.

"Nicholas, don't you look dapper this morning," exclaimed Lady Darby. "I'm glad you could join us."

He gave his mother a wry look before finding Hannah. "Good morning, my lady," he said with a bow.

She smiled and stood to fill her plate. "Happy Christmas, Nicholas. I do hope you feel well this morning?" Her eyes remained on the silver tray as she scooped eggs and a piece of toasted bread onto her plate.

"Yes, as a matter of fact, I feel wonderful." He moved next to her and picked up a plate. "You look lovely. Emerald green suits you. It turns your hair to a dark honey."

Hannah turned and looked him in the eye. "Do you remember last night?"

His mouth opened, closed, then opened again. "Yes, of course." He continued with a whisper, "Most of it, I think."

She whispered back, "Most of it? We will have to find out later which part you've forgotten." Then she gave him a bright smile and walked away.

The breakfast was delicious and the conversation lively.

"The room is perfect!" Hannah admired the greenery and ribbons and beads. "Is the wassail ready for this afternoon?"

"Yes. I think everything is prepared." Mattie poured her brother some coffee. "Was your family upset, Hannah? I saw the letter arrive."

She shook her head. "They are disappointed, as was I, but they are happy I am well and in good company. I miss my little step-niece Althea the most, I think. She's so full of joy."

"I always wanted a sister," Mattie said wistfully. "Not that there is anything wrong with a brother."

"Oh no, they can be wonderful," agreed Hannah. "But I always longed for a sister too. Thea is adorable but I'm so grateful for my sister-in-law, Eliza. We are as close as if we'd been born to the same family."

Nicholas listened and smiled to himself. Mattie would get her wish for Christmas.

"Lady Darby, if you don't mind, an old friend will be stopping by today to share some wassail."

"Of course," said the countess, though her smile was tight. "Who shall I expect?"

"Lord Chester Hatford. We met in India years ago and came across one another at the masquerade ball."

"Lord Chester? His brother is the marquess?" The shock on Lady Darby's face seemed to have the effect Lady Roberta had hoped for.

"Yes," she said smugly, "we are great friends. Had some monstrous adventures together."

"Do you have any visits to make, Mother?" asked Nicholas. He wouldn't mind her out of the house for an hour or two this afternoon.

"I do. I am expected at a friend's at three. I will be home in time for the festivities Mattie has planned." She gave him a pointed look.

Nicholas understood. His mother's "friend" would be Alice's mother. Her name had not been mentioned in five years. He still wasn't ready to forgive that conspiracy, but today he felt as if it might be a future possibility. The world seemed a happier place today.

"You play beautifully, Mattie. I wish I had the patience for the harp," said Hannah. "The pianoforte is struggle enough."

"I must disagree. I hated finding the right key, and the terrible sound when I hit the wrong chord. I find the strings much easier." Mattie turned toward the door where Nicholas stood under the threshold.

"In or out, dear brother?"

"That depends. Miss Pendleton, might I have a word?" He tried to arrange his face in a serious expression, lest she guess his motive.

Hannah nodded and met him at the door. "Is it about last night?" she whispered.

"No, it's about traditions. This is one of mine." He pointed up at the mistletoe and grinned.

She looked up, then back at his face, understanding showing in her eyes. With a smile, she closed her eyes and tilted her face, waiting. He dipped his head and brushed his lips against hers. Egad, the power of those lips. Did she have any idea?

He plucked a berry from the bough. She turned away, and he caught her hand, pulling her back. She blushed, her eyes shining with anticipation as he bent down again. This time he lingered, breathing in the intoxicating apricot. Then he plucked another berry from the bough.

"Leave some for the others, brother," teased Mattie.

"Not you, I daresay," he said as sternly as he could, still feeling the blood rushing through his veins from Hannah's kisses.

"I'm thinking of Lady Roberta and her new beau."

"How do you know he's a beau?" asked Nicholas. "I don't recall her mentioning it."

"They were involved years ago in India. I don't think Aunt Bertie was ready to get married. She didn't want a man getting in the way of her travels." Hannah shrugged. "But now that she's older, and he's a widower, well… Love doesn't count the years."

"No, I suppose not. Your aunt is a good woman. She deserves to find love." Nicholas sat down in front of the hearth. "Mattie, do you suppose Hannah and I might have a word alone?"

"Well, we were just going to—" She looked from her brother to her friend and nodded slowly. "Yes, I'll go check on the wassail."

Nicholas walked to the hearth and fingered a gold ribbon in the greenery. "Hannah, I must apologize for last night. I wasn't in my right mind when—"

"You said you loved me?"

Heat rose from his neck to his face. Blast! This was not going as planned. "I said that?"

"Obviously one of the parts that escaped your memory," she said with a blank face.

What was she thinking? Was she furious? Glad? Might as well jump right in. No use mincing words.

"I meant it, Hannah, with all my heart." His stomach clenched as she strode to him, a stern expression on her beautiful features.

In the dancing firelight, her eyes shone as gold as the ribbon. "You were drunk as a wheelbarrow. I didn't like it."

That was to the point. "I know it wasn't the best impression. It was a…final farewell to my past."

"And Alice?"

His pulse raced. "Yes. I need to explain about my first marriage." He closed his eyes. How could he tell her the past five years had been hell, and he'd been an empty shell with only one goal. How could he find the words to make her see she had filled that hollow place that alcohol never could?

"I read the letter, Nicholas. I didn't mean to pry, but it fell from your hand. When I picked it up, I… Well, I'm only human." She laid a palm on his cheek. "I am concerned that this will always be between us."

He shook his head. "I never loved her. You are the only one to steal my heart. Because of you, I don't need the brandy to fall asleep. Because of you, the nightmares are fewer and fewer. I need you, Hannah. With my every breath, I need you."

"Oh, Nicholas, it's not your affection for me that gives me pause. It's your conscience. We will never be happy if you have not forgiven yourself for her death. Her words haunted me all night, so I can only imagine how they have plagued you." She withdrew her hand, and he stopped himself from grabbing it to his chest. "I must know you can think of the past without the burden of guilt. It was not your fault. None of it. You were as much a victim as poor Alice."

He blinked at the moisture in his eyes. His throat was swollen and he tried to swallow, tried to say something. *By Christ, you can't cry.* With an effort, he pushed back the emotion.

"Last night was the anniversary of her death, our wedding. It's the first time I've returned to that room. I had it in my mind that I needed to return there to tell her. Tell her it was done, Colvin would be punished, and justice administered. Perhaps not by my hand, but he will never hurt an innocent again." He took a deep breath. "Today, I feel like a new man. This is a new beginning for me. *You* are my chance to start again."

He dropped to one knee. "Miss Hannah Pendleton, will you do me the great honor of becoming my wife?"

Her eyes glistened, her smile tremulous. "Yes, Lord Darby, I will marry you."

He stood and cupped her face in his hands. "I may have rescued you earlier this week, but you have rescued me from a lifetime of misery."

He kissed her, closing his eyes when her velvet lips met his. He pulled her against him, feeling how her curves fit against his like the pieces of a puzzle. With her, he was whole again. Her hands went from his shoulders, tracing the curve of his arm, and up his chest.

Desire stoked deep inside him, and he felt his passion grow. His tongue glided along the seam of her mouth, begging to delve deeper, and she opened to him. She tasted of gingerbread and fresh butter and he wanted to devour her, every inch of her.

"Nicholas," she said against his lips, "I think—"

"Don't," he said and moved his attention to her jaw, trailing kisses down her neck.

She tipped her head back, and a soft moan escaped her throat. He chuckled, feeling himself harden with the thought of the sounds she would make another time. His lips traced her collarbone. She pushed on his chest.

"Nicholas," she whispered, "I think we have an audience."

His head jerked up. In the doorway stood a grinning Lady Roberta and Lord Chester.

"Well," exclaimed Lord Chester, "it looks like love is the theme for this Christmas, eh?"

Lady Roberta chuckled. "Did you propose, Lord Darby? Or are you taking advantage of my niece under my nose?"

"We are betrothed, Aunt Bertie, never fear. Not that propriety has ever been a major concern of yours." Hannah laughed when Lady Roberta flapped her arms at the comment.

"Propriety would never have gotten me the love of my life, now would it?" she asked with a wink, then looked up at Lord Chester. "My dear, do you see where we are standing?"

He looked up and grinned. "My, my, it *is* my lucky day."

With that, the older gentleman put his arms about Lady Roberta's waist and kissed her with all the passion of a young man. Nicholas whistled. "I'm glad to know age does not dampen ardor."

"Not if it's the right one, my boy. Not if it's the right one."

Nicholas turned back to Hannah. "Happy Christmas, my love." He bent to kiss her and she put her fingers on his lips.

"What about the mistletoe? Shouldn't we wait for our turn?"

"To hell with the mistletoe, and to hell with waiting." And with that, he claimed her lips and any further protests. He'd have to sneak some more berries in the bough when no one was looking. It was going to be a lusty holiday and numerous kisses between now and Twelfth Night.

AFTERWORD

When my editor first received this story, she called me. "You're beginning a Christmas story with a suicide?" She asked in a worried tone. I explained in order to understand the hero, we had to experience why he was so driven. I promised her I would make it work, and in the end, she was surprised and pleased.

I wanted to dedicate this to the many who do not enjoy the holidays. To those who anticipate the season with dread, know they will succumb to depression, and avoid the well-meaning friends who try to rally them with good cheer. We lost my mother-in-law in December, and it was difficult to have the same joy without her.

Though time often heals, we cannot move the hands of that abstract clock to suit our own needs. Patience and love are the keys to supporting a loved one dealing with depression or any mental health issues.

In the end, Nicholas, Earl of Darby, found his needed comfort with the passage of time, the hand of justice, and in the arms of Hannah. I hope you found the end joyful, restorative, and romantic enough to overcome the prologue.

I'll also share a secret. Lady Matilda's story will be next in the Once Upon a Widow series. The pirate she danced with at the masquerade ball? None other than the ex-Bow Street Runner, Walters!

Fact Check:

The Cato Street Conspiracy was a true event. It was an attempt by radicals to revive the spirit of the French Revolution. While it is not known how widespread the conspiracy was, the rumors were numerous. An informer helped the police trap the plotters at their Cato Street meeting place near Edgware Road in London.

The original conspirators were known as the Spencean Philanthropists, named after the British radical, Thomas Spence. Some of them had taken part in the earlier Spa Field Riots of 1816, still incensed by the Six Acts and Peterloo Massacre (described in *Rhapsody and Rebellion*).

The plan: assassinate the cabinet while they were gathered at a dinner. Then the Philanthropists would overthrow the government by capturing key buildings and form a "Committee of Public Safety." Unfortunately for the conspirators, there was a spy among them. He created the fictitious dinner where the officials would be murdered and financed the plot. In my story, I have used the evil duke as the source of those funds provided by the spy.

Arrests were made on February 23, 1820. On May 1 at Newgate Prison, the convicted were hanged in front of a crowd of thousands. They were strung up for half an hour before being cut down and decapitated, each head shown to the crowd and denounced as the head of a traitor before being placed in the coffin next to their bodies.

I thought this would be a fitting end for my villain, the Duke of Colvin, and fitting justice for poor Alice.

Earl of Scarborough
  The Honorable Rogues
  Wicked Earls' Club
  By
  Collette Cameron

October 1817
  Wicked Earls' Club, London England

Bored. Bored. Bored.

Ansley Twistleton, the Earl of Scarborough, was bored. Out of his mind with *ennui*. Furthermore, he had absolutely no bloody idea, whatsoever, how to remedy the situation. This discontentment. This restlessness. This new, entirely irksome, wholly vexing dissatisfaction. It made him edgy and irritable.

As was his habit, he analyzed his feelings logically and dispassionately. To a degree, he'd brought this state of malaise on himself. A man of rigid schedules and habits, nothing unexpected or exciting ever happened to him. That was precisely how he preferred his well-ordered, predictable life.

Until now.

Drumming his fingertips atop his thigh, he clamped his back teeth together, pondering the exasperating irregularity.

Why now? Why, after years of consistency, was he bored?

Probably, because his pursuits and interests were few.

He neither gambled nor frequented bordellos—*God only knew how many men those creatures of the boudoir had serviced*—nor did he racehorses. Assemblies, routs, balls, and the like were avoided like the plague or clap, as were picnics, the opera, musicals, and the theater.

Although... He'd been known to attend the latter by himself. If the play consisted of something worth watching, and he made his way into his box before anyone had a chance to corner him into conversation. There was the inconvenience of having to wait until most of the other patrons had departed before he could make his escape. But on rare occasions, the performance had been entertaining enough to warrant the minor irritation.

To say he was socially awkward was as much an under-statement as suggesting Caroline of Brunswick was out of favor with the portly Prince Regent, or the English had a slight partiality for tea.

Ansley's physical fitness and athleticism could be contributed to hours spent riding, fencing, and biweekly bouts of training at No.13 Bond Street with Jackson himself. Generally, those activities required little more than an occa-sional one-syllable-word comment, a grunt, or a noncom-mittal noise in the back of his throat.

Men never felt the need to blather on just to hear their own voices. And of colossal more importance, no primping, simpering, *salivating* females were ever in attendance.

God, help him. But like hounds on the fresh scent of

blood, eligible young misses, their terrifying marriage-minded mamas, and their pernicious plotting papas had the habit of popping up at the most inopportune moments.

Much like disease-infested rats, cockroaches, or fleas.

One knew the loathsome pests lurked about in dark corners and crevices, but when one accidentally came upon one, the experience proved most alarming and unpleasant. Unlike *those* vermin which usually ended up dead, the giggling debutantes—God's bones how he detested giggling —were almost certain to appear again.

And again. *And again.* God help him and any other unattached male possessing a title.

Fingering his glass with its remaining dram of superior cognac, he rested his head against the wingback chair's plush crimson velvet. Legs crossed at the ankles, he stretched them before him and stared at the robust fire through half-closed eyelids.

Around him, the soft din of his fellow Wicked Earls' Club members' gaming, laughter, and conversations barely permeated his aura of jaded disinterest.

A wry smile kicked his lips up on one side. *Wicked earls, indeed.* His claims to wickedness were his cutting, sardonic tongue and wit. However, he couldn't vouch for the other earls one way or the other. He didn't know any of them well enough to form an opinion.

The trouble was, he decided, returning to the issue of his boredom with a slight downward slant of his mouth and a drink of the amber liquid, he eschewed most social gatherings. Consequently, he often found himself with nothing at all to do.

Until recently, that truth hadn't bothered him. He'd even declined to seek memberships at White's, Brooks, and Boodle's. As select as those gentlemen clubs were, they still allowed far too many members for his comfort.

Other than the secret Wicked Earls' Club and *Bon Chance* —another exclusive club and the only two places other than his country estate where he felt a degree of ease around other people—he avoided *le beau monde*.

Well, he didn't *willingly* entertain and mingle with the *haut ton*.

Since coming into his title seven years ago at the tender age of one and twenty, due to the premature death of his uncle, he'd been obligated to venture out on occasion. Very rare occasions. Mostly when his mother or sister entreated him to put on a mien of civilization. And loving them as much as he did, he tried to oblige their wishes every now and again.

He suspected they were the only two people entirely aware of what an immense effort it took each time to don his public persona. For he couldn't bear changes in his routines. Most particularly, unforeseen variations.

It rattled him in a way that was not only difficult to explain, but disconcerting and humiliating. Everything in his ordered life had a time. When he rose. Bathed. When he ate. What time he retired. When his hair was trimmed—every third Wednesday at half-past two. When he arrived at his clubs and, unsurprisingly, when he departed.

More than once, he'd wondered if he was even sane.

Surely such compulsions bordered on madness. A terrifying notion that had haunted him since his youth.

At least he wasn't as dotty as that fellow who put on and removed his shoes five times before he'd leave his home and then checked to make sure the door was soundly locked by pushing the handle then the door itself in rapid succession four times.

No one—*bloody no one*—kept to habits as he did. Several times, he'd tried to ease his inflexibility and found himself a wreck. Tense. His nerves on edge. Unable to concentrate or relax. His oddity was a damn curse. Indeed, it was.

Oh, he could do it—if push came to shove. In fact, typically, no one was the wiser except those closest to him. But he preferred not to stray from routine if at all possible.

He dragged his eyes open and squinted at the white marble and gilt bronze clock. Exhaling a long breath, he levered himself upright in the chair and tossed back the remaining spirits. Time to leave. He set the glass aside, then shoved to his feet.

No one paid him much mind, which didn't bother him in the least. He enjoyed solitude. Craved it, in fact. He'd wanted to be a scholar before inheriting the earldom—had hoped to teach Natural History and Ecclesiastical History at Oxford or Cambridge.

But earls didn't don austere robes and become professors. A rather irritating voice also dared remind him he mightn't have been able to stand before a hall of students and orate.

God's teeth. His own education had been as painful as hell, and he couldn't deny the truth. Despite his desire to teach, he lacked the wherewithal. No, that wasn't precisely correct. He possessed the knowledge but was without the ability to adequately communicate with or instruct a room full of pupils.

Reclining against the back of his usual chair beside the window, the Earl of Alcott smoked a cigar and stared morosely into his whisky tumbler. Somber, sad even, he raised the hand with the cigar toward Ansley in a silent farewell.

He acknowledged the salute with an elevated chin. Alcott was a decent chap. In fact, it was he who suggested Ansley join the Wicked Earls' Club.

Nonetheless, he hadn't ventured to the club tonight for titillating conversation. Or any other night, for that matter.

Not a bit of it. No, he forced himself out of his rather osten-tatious Grosvenor Square house four nights a week, else he'd easily become a hermit, locked inside his comfortable home, playing the pianoforte, wasting time on billiards, and reading musty old tomes till time for bed.

Sounded like bloody bliss.

Another sardonic twist of his mouth followed his retro-spection.

He rather liked the thought, truth be told. Why, he wouldn't even be required to shave or even dress, for that matter. All his meals might be taken in his banyan.

Recalling the correspondence from his mother this morning, *suggesting* the names of several eligible young misses that would make *"exceptionally, wonderful countesses,"* the tic near his left eye began twitching in earnest. A sure indication he was more upset than his outward façade of bored-nonchalance proclaimed. One would think he'd have become accustomed to the spasms, yet deep-rooted humilia-tion tumbled about in his stomach.

Dearest Mama had also recommended he host a Christ-mastide house party this year at Fawtonbrooke Hall, his country estate. He barely suppressed a shudder of distaste.

Horror of absolutely absurd horrors.

Guests tramping all about his sanctuary from dawn to midnight or later? Required to dine with them? Entertain the throng? Converse. *Dance?*

Absolutely not.

Bright-eyed misses with their coy smiles and simpering manners.

Hell on earth. A fate worse than death for a man like himself.

The muscle by his eye convulsed harder, and he angled his head toward the fireplace to hide the tremor lest it draw unsolicited attention. Disgust and anger at himself that he could yet be self-conscious of his—*inconvenience*—jabbed his pride.

Mama simply could not accept that at eight and twenty—nine and twenty in January—he possessed as much desire to wed as he did to have all of his teeth pulled. *Or be keelhauled. Tarred and feathered. Eviscerated with a hairpin. Burned at the stake. Hung by his ballocks.*

A wife dragging him hither and yon, chattering like a magpie about nonsensical drivel, would drive him stark-raving mad. And what kind of a spouse would he be? Other than his title and passably good looks, he held no false illusions about his appeal or qualifications as a husband.

Or lack thereof.

In short, Ansley Cecil Huxley Twistleton, sixth Earl of Scarborough, was a stuffy, dour chap who broke into a cold sweat when in a room with more than a dozen or so people. A man who had as much skill with small talk as he did needlepoint or midwifery. A lord who'd been thrust into a life he had no more aptitude for than a hippopotamus did for ballet, or a cat for archery.

He was an oddity.

And, blast and damn, he shouldn't care.

Want to read more of Ansley and Willow's romance?
Get EARL OF SCARBOROUGH at major retailers!

ABOUT THE AUTHOR

Bestselling and award-winning author Aubrey Wynne is an elementary teacher by trade, champion of children and animals by conscience, and author by night. She resides in the Midwest with her husband, dogs, horses, mule, and barn cats. Obsessions include wine, history, travel, trail riding, and all things Christmas. Her Chicago Christmas series has received the Golden Quill, Aspen Gold, Heart of Excellence, and the Gayle Wilson Award of Excellence and twice nominated as a Rone finalist by InD'tale Magazine.

Aubrey's first love is medieval romance but after dipping her toe in the Regency period in 2018 with the *Wicked Earls' Club,* she was smitten. This inspired her award-winning series *Once Upon a Widow.* In 2020, she will launch the Scottish Regency series *A MacNaughton Castle Romance* with Dragonblade Novels.

Social Media Links:
  Website:
  http://www.aubreywynne.com
  Aubrey's Ever After Facebook group:
  https://www.facebook.com/
groups/AubreyWynnesEverAfters/
  Sign up for my newsletter and don't miss future releases
  https://www.subscribepage.com/k3f1z5

MORE HISTORICAL ROMANCE

Once Upon a Widow (Sweet Regency Series)

Earl of Sunderland #1

Maggie award, International Digital Awards finalist

Grace Beaumont has seen what love can do to a woman. Her mother sacrificed her life to produce the coveted son and heir. A devastated father and newborn brother force her to take on the role of Lady Boldon at the age of fifteen. But Grace finds solace in the freedom and power of her new status.

Christopher Roker made a name for himself in the military. The rigor and pragmatism of the army suits him. When a tragic accident heaves Kit into a role he never wanted or expected, his world collides with another type of duty. Returning to England and his newfound responsibilities, the Wicked Earls' Club becomes a refuge from the glitter and malice of London society but cannot ease his emptiness.

Needing an escape from his late brother's memory and reputation, Kit visits the family estate for the summer. Lady

Grace, a beauty visiting from a neighboring estate, becomes a welcome distraction. When the chance to return to the military becomes a valid possibility, the earl finds himself wavering between his old life and the lure of an exceptional —and unwilling—woman.

A Wicked Earl's Widow #2

Eliza is forced into marriage with no idea her life will change for the better. Married less than a year, her unwilling rake of a husband is surprisingly kind to her—until his sudden death. The widowed Countess of Sunderland remains under her in-laws' protection to raise her newborn daughter. But her abusive father is on the brink of financial ruin and has plans for another wedding.

Nathaniel, Viscount of Pendleton, gains his title at the age of twelve. His kindly but shrewd estate manager becomes father and mentor, instilling in the boy an astute sense of responsibility and compassion for his tenants. Fifteen years later, his family urges him to visit London and seek a wife. The ideal doesn't appeal to him, but his sense of duty tells him it is the next logical step.

Lord Pendleton stumbles upon Eliza on the road, defending an elderly woman against ruffians

After rescuing the exquisite damsel in distress, he finds himself smitten. But Nate soon realizes he must discover the dark secrets of her past to truly save the woman he loves.

Rhapsody and Rebellion Book #3

Maggie finalist, nominated for Rone Award, InD'tale Magazine

A Scottish legacy... A political rebellion... Two hearts destined to meet...

Raised in his father's image, the Earl of Stanfeld is practical and disciplined. There are no gray lines interrupting the Gideon's black and white world. Until his mother has a dream and begs to return to her Highland home.

Alisabeth was betrothed from the cradle. At seventeen, she marries her best friend and finds happiness if not passion. In less than a year, a political rebellion makes her a widow. The handsome English earl arrives a month later and rouses her desire and a terrible guilt.

Crossing the border into Scotland, Gideon finds his predictable world turned upside down. Folklore, legend, and political unrest intertwine with an unexpected attraction to a feisty Highland beauty. When the earl learns of an English plot to stir the Scots into rebellion, he must choose his country or save the clan and the woman who stirs his soul.

Earl of Darby #4

Miss Hannah Pendleton is nursing her pride after her childhood crush falls in love with another. Determined to break a few hearts of her own, she hurls herself into the exciting and hectic schedule of a first season. Always clever and direct, the smooth manners and practiced words of the gallant but meticulous bachelors do nothing to stir her soul until...

Since his wife's suicide on their wedding night, the Earl of Darby has carefully cultivated his rakish reputation. It keeps overprotective mamas at bay and provides him with unlimited clandestine affairs. But when Nicholas sees a lovely newcomer being courted by the devil himself, her innocence and candor revive the chivalry buried deep in his soul. The ice around Nicholas's heart cracks as he desperately tries to save Hannah and right a hideous wrong committed so long ago.

A Medieval Encounter Series

Rolf's Quest

Great Expectations winner, Fire & Ice, Maggie finalist

"Romance, destiny, family values & betrayal all played parts in this intriguing novel that had me turning each page in anticipation."

The BookTweeter

"I enjoyed the flow of the story and the sweet, charming romance. There were unexpected twists and turns that kept my pages turning until the very last page! I highly recommend taking a read through Aubrey's tapestry of Merlin, magic, and true love."

Verified Purchase Review

A wizard, a curse, a fated love...

When Rolf finally discovers the woman who can end the curse that has plagued his family for centuries, she is already betrothed. Time is running out for the royal wizard of King Henry II. If he cannot find true love without the use of sorcery, the magic will die for future generations.

Melissa is intrigued by the mystical, handsome man who haunts her by night and tempts her by day. His bizarre tale of Merlin, enchantments, and finding genuine love has her questioning his sanity and her heart.

From the moment Melissa stepped from his dreams and into his arms, Rolf knew she was his destiny. Now, he will battle against time, a powerful duke, and call on the gods to save her.

Saving Grace (A Small Town Romance)

Contemporary and Colonial America

Holt and Maggie finalist

This unique piece has the reader traveling between the early 1700s and the early 2000s with ease and amazement. The audience truly feels sorrow for Grace and Chloe and is able to connect with each woman for the hardships they are over-coming… The attention to historical facts and details leave one breathless, especially upon learning the people from the past did exist and the memorial erected still stands.

InD'tale Magazine

"I am becoming a pretty decent fan of the author I would say at this point. She managed in such a short amount of pages to thrill me with some lore, romance, and suspense."

Verified Purchase Review

A tortured soul meets a shattered heart...

Chloe Hicks' life consisted of an egocentric ex-husband, a pile of bills, and an equine business in foreclosure until a fire destroys the stable and her beloved ranch horse. What little hope she has left is smashed after the marshal suspects arson. She escapes the accusing eyes of her hometown, but not the memories and melancholy.

Jackson Hahn, Virginia Beach's local historian, has his eyes on the mysterious new woman in town. When she enters his office, he is struck by her haunting beauty and the raw pain in her eyes. Her descriptions of the odd events happening in her bungalow pique his curiosity.

The sexy historian distracts Chloe with the legend of a woman wrongly accused of witchcraft. She is drawn to the story and the similarities of events that plagued their lives. Perhaps the past can help heal the present. But danger lurks in the shadows...

A Chicago Christmas (Sweet Holiday Novella Series)

Dante's Gift

(Chicago Christmas #1)
Contemporary and WWII

Winner of the Golden Quill, Aspen Gold and Heart of Excellence RWA awards, Rone Award finalist in Audio

"Wynne has crafted a beautiful short story guaranteed to warm your heart and make you sigh."

Kishan Paul, *Second Wife Series*

"...a wonderfully poignant holiday romantic tale that intertwines two love stories..."

Jersey Girls Book Reviews

"A lovely sweet romance!"

Book Addicts

Kathleen James has put her practical side away for once and looks forward to the perfect romantic evening: an intimate dinner with the man of her dreams—and an engagement ring. She is not prepared to hear that he wants to bring his grandmother back from Italy to live with him.

Dominic Lawrence has planned this marriage proposal for six months. Nothing can go wrong— until his Nonna calls. Now he must interrupt the tenderest night of Katie's life with the news that another woman will be under their roof.

When Antonia's sister dies, she finds herself

longing to be back in the states. An Italian wartime bride from the '40s, she knows how precious love can be. Can her own story of an American soldier and a very special collie once again bring two hearts together at Christmas?

For the Love of Laura Beth (Chicago Christmas #4)

2019 Rone Finalist, InD'Tale Magazine

Book Buyers Best award, Maggie and International Digital Awards finalist

"Beautifully written and tells a story that will allow readers to experience the turmoil that war can bring to the lives of those who must endure its heartbreak."

Verified Purchase Review

"This isn't your typical boy-meets-girl-they-get-married-and-live-happily-ever-after-the-end story. This is sweet romance in the midst of real life hardships and pain, and a love that will press through and triumph."

Verified Purchase Review

The Korean War destroyed their plans, but the battle at home may shatter their hearts...

Laura Beth Walters fell in love with Joe McCall when she was six years old. Now she is counting the days until Joey graduates from college so they can marry and begin their life together. But the Korean War rips their neatly laid plans to shreds. Instead of a college fraternity, Joey joins a platoon. Laura Beth trades a traditional wedding for a quick trip to the courthouse.

They endure the hardships of separation, but the true battle is faced when Joey returns from the war. Their devotion is soon tested beyond endurance. Joe and Laura Beth must find a way to accept the trials thrown in their path and remain steadfast, or lose their faith and each other.

80513536R00100